T0374230

The Wrong Side of Life

The Wrong Side of Life

GORDON DONNELL

THE WRONG SIDE OF LIFE

iUniverse books may be ordered through booksellers or by contacting:

iUniverse
1663 Liberty Drive
Bloomington, IN 47403
www.iuniverse.com
844-349-9409

Because of the dynamic nature of the Internet, any web addresses or links contained in this book may have changed since publication and may no longer be valid. The views expressed in this work are solely those of the author and do not necessarily reflect the views of the publisher, and the publisher hereby disclaims any responsibility for them.

Any people depicted in stock imagery provided by Getty Images are models, and such images are being used for illustrative purposes only. Certain stock imagery © Getty Images.

ISBN: 978-1-6632-6530-2 (sc)
ISBN: 978-1-6632-6531-9 (e)

Library of Congress Control Number: 2024915361

Print information available on the last page.

iUniverse rev. date: 07/22/2024

Introduction

This is a work of noir fiction. Its purpose is to provide escapist entertainment. The characters are fictitious. References to actual events are made only to establish historical context.

The work consists of stories arranged chronologically to provide glimpses into the dark side of American culture as it has evolved over many decades. The people are ordinary and in no way heroic. Their stories are self-contained and conveniently brief. The reader can put aside the routine of life and enjoy a trip back in time whenever a few minutes become available.

A word of caution: The characters and events are viewed through the lens of their time, and no allowance is made for current sensitivities in either attitudes or the language in which they are presented.

Real Men

i

I'd driven my route. Turned in the cash. Made the entries for the horses, the numbers, the sports bets. It wasn't so bad what I did. This was 1955. People were going to bet. It wasn't my fault. It was just my upbringing nagging me to do the right thing.

Yeah. Sure.

I learned better in Korea. I learned it carrying kids who did the right thing to Graves Registration. No speeches. No medals. No bugle playing Taps. Just four of you lugging what was left of a buddy on a poncho. Knowing next time it could be you.

I was lucky. I got out with a Purple Heart and a bum leg. I got out knowing there was no such thing as tomorrow. Grab today. Get what you can.

My street was just off Wilshire. High fashion maybe twenty years ago. I parked in the garage under my apartment building and dug the Colt out of the glove box.

The gun was just protection. My route took me into scary neighborhoods. Cars got prowled sometimes, so I always took it in with me.

There were two people arguing in the elevator vestibule. They stopped and stared when I came in.

I had seen the woman in the building. I had never talked to her. Her looks put her way out of my league.

The man was heavy. Handsome. Snappy dresser. He was looking at my hand. I realized I was still holding the Colt. I hadn't put it in my pocket.

"Who are you supposed to be?" he snarled.

"The guy with the gun," I said.

"That supposed to mean something?"

"You're making trouble where I live," I said. "Trouble causes cops."

The sneer in his eyes said he wasn't impressed. "You trying to tell me you work for Mickey Cohen?"

"Only Mickey Cohen I know drives a school bus," I said.

He didn't like that. Cohen was in Federal Prison. McNeil Island. He still ran the bad stuff in LA. Everybody knew it. The only people with anything to gain denying it were people who actually did work for him.

"Beat it," I said, before Beefy Boy had time to do any serious thinking.

Thinking didn't seem to be one of his strong points. He sidled out of the vestibule and went to an old Cadillac. It took him that long to come up with an idea. He flipped me the finger and drove off.

The woman was gone by then. I hadn't heard the elevator, but it was pretty quiet.

I looked at the gun in my hand and a shiver ran through me. If Beefy Boy had been a cop, I'd be wearing handcuffs. From now on, I'd leave it in the car.

ii

She was waiting for me when I got home the next night. The woman from the vestibule. She sat on the sofa, showing me more leg than women usually showed me.

"Your door wasn't locked," she said. Her voice was low, husky. "So I came in to wait."

The door had been locked. I double-checked when I left. I'm funny that way. Going back to make sure I didn't leave a light on or water running.

"Buy you a drink?" I asked.

"You're a bag man for Snake-Eyes Fletcher," she said.

After Korea I finished accounting school on the GI Bill. A guy I knew from the Army knew people who were looking for somebody good with numbers. When you're a gimp with paper from a no-name college, you don't get a lot of offers. Okay, so I was a bag man.

I had never met Fletcher. I hadn't seen him but a few times. A trim, cold, dapper man who kept to his business.

"I think he likes to be called Jack," I said.

The woman just laughed. I could feel her in my hip pocket, and she knew it.   I made my way to a chair wishing my limp wasn't so obvious.

"What's your name?" I asked.

"How much do you pick up every night?" she asked. "Money, I mean."

Twenty three stops. A bag from each. Fletcher's operation was above a downtown garage, where cars coming and going wouldn't be noticed. A quiet place to do the processing. Sort the bills by denomination. Make the entries. Total and cross check.

"How much depends on what's going on," I said. "If there's not much to bet on, it's not so much."

"It's a lot," she said, "or they wouldn't have someone pick it up every night."

"If you say so."

"Ever think about just driving off with it one night? Getting lost and never coming back?"

"No," I lied.

"A real man would think of that," she said.

"I wouldn't get to the city limits."

"What if you got robbed?" she asked. "You know, hit over the head, so it wasn't your fault."

"How long have you been married?" I asked.

She held up her left hand and inspected an empty ring finger. Tan lines revealed the truth.

"You and Beefy Boy," I said. "How long?"

She didn't answer.

"Fletcher isn't a fool," I said.

"You are."

The husky voice was full of contempt. She was on her feet and gone, just like that. She had tried me out and I had disappointed her.

I moved to the sofa where her fragrance lingered. The cushions were still warm. It wasn't much, but it was all I was going to get.

iii

It's funny, the tricks your mind plays on you. One night a woman I didn't know talked about driving off with the take. The next night I could feel eyes on me at every stop on the route.

There were some stops where I wasn't surprised by the feeling. Parts of the city where it was real. Streets where neon flickered and sizzled over bars and pool halls. Where the sidewalk loafers saw everything without seeming to look at anything.

It didn't spook me until I started feeling it on the streets where there were no stops. Empty streets where the wind raised miniature dust devils in the headlight beams and the street lamps made gargoyles out of the eucalyptus trees.

After that everyone seemed to be watching. Even the old couple who ran the hole-in-the-wall grocery store. They seemed like nice people. My guess was their percentage of Fletcher's action was the difference between razor thin profits and receivership.

The people at the greasy spoons, they weren't so nice. Worn out souls who hunkered in the booths and tried to nurse a few extra vitamins out of the free coffee refill while they dreamed about getting a break. Any break. Even a little one.

In places like that everyone knew everyone and even a ripple in the routine got noticed fast.

Everyone knew my car. They couldn't miss it. Flashy new Ford. Two tone. Raven Black and Goldenrod Yellow.

Everyone knew I worked for Fletcher. They knew what time I showed up. They knew how I acted when I did. Who I talked to and what I said.

I made sure I hit every location exactly on my normal time. Parked exactly where I normally parked. Made the same conversation with the same people. Just so nobody would get the idea anything was wrong.

Fletcher kept guys on the payroll to make sure things didn't go wrong. And to do something about it when they did.

I had heard stories about the guy who had the route before me. There were questions about him. Nobody ever said what the questions were. One night he wasn't there anymore. Not a peep out of anyone. He was just gone. No one ever saw him again.

He made a mistake. Maybe a big one. Maybe just a little one. Someone on the route spotted it and ratted him out. It was like the route was jinxed. Like I had moved into a haunted house.

My last stop was Lonnie's Lanes. A bowling alley down where a lot of Okies lived. I pulled around in back, parked like usual.

It was quiet there. Dark except for the light over the service door. A stray cat arched its back and hissed at me from the lid of a garbage can when I got out of the car.

An acne scarred runt opened the service door and let me into a clatter of falling pins and a howl of hillbilly music from the jukebox. Stale tobacco smoke poisoned the air. It was stifling, but still not enough to mask the smell of food from the cafe.

The place put an edge on my nerves. It always had. I could never put a finger on why.

Okay, so maybe it was all in my head. Like the nightmares. The ones that left me shaking and drenched in sweat. Like never being able to push the bad stuff from Korea out of my memory. I was still glad to get back to Fletcher's garage.

No more jumping at shadows.

iv

She was waiting for me when I got home. Sitting where she sat the night before, in just the same way. She made a neat distraction.

My only warning was a whiff of man's cologne, and then I was down on my knees, doubled up in pain and gasping for air. I heard the door close and felt hands in my pockets.

"Where's the gun?"

I remembered the voice from the elevator vestibule. She had brought Beefy Boy this time.

"Forget it, Marty," she said. "If he hasn't got it, he hasn't got it."

Marty grabbed the lapels of my sport coat and hauled me to something resembling a standing position.

"Think you can take me?" he demanded.

I could barely breathe, let alone answer.

"I used to fight," he said. "Light heavy. Sure, a couple guys took me in the ring, but they were good. They were contenders. Nobody ever took me on the street."

He was mad at me. I had scared him with the gun. He had backed off in front of his wife, and now he was mad at me.

He hit me a short jab in the stomach. The woman stood and came over.

"He can't do us any good if you kill him," she said. "Just give him the set up."

"There's a fight tomorrow," he told me. "Twelve rounds. Big build-up in the papers. You heard about it?"

I managed to shake my head.

"Swede fighting a shine. Big money on a fight like that. Lots of action."

I nodded. Not for any reason. It just seemed like a good idea.

The woman was getting impatient. She took over.

"Your last stop is a bowling alley. You park in back. Just like tonight. Leave the keys in the car. When you come out, Marty clips you. Just enough so when they find you, you're out cold and the car is gone."

It was stupid. I was going to tell her it wouldn't work when Marty drove another jab into my stomach.

"You got that?"

"That's enough, Marty," the woman said. "I'll take it from here."

She shooed him out and helped me to a chair.

"He gets crazy," she said. "He'll kill us both if you don't go through with it."

The pain churning in my gut made that a convincing argument.

"I'll make it up to you afterward," she promised.

She kissed my cheek before she left.

v

The next night my gut was still sore where Marty had slugged me, and

I could still feel his wife's kiss on my cheek. I left on my route without telling anyone at Fletcher's garage what had happened.

Marty and his wife would call me a liar. Fletcher's guys wouldn't know who to believe. When they didn't know who to believe, they didn't believe anyone. That's when things could get ugly.

Calling in sick wouldn't have done me any good. If I didn't show at Lonnie's, Marty would pick his time and finish what he started.

I had only one way to go. Drive the route. Take what came.

It was like Korea. Like the night patrols. Knowing something bad was waiting for you. Knowing there wasn't a damn thing you could do about it.

Marty was right about the action on the fight.

"All day they been coming in," the Polack behind the bar at my first stop told me.

The bag he handed over was fat. Heavier than usual.

"Guys who never bet more than a buck got down for five."

He said it like it was the eighth wonder of the world.

"The regular five buck players," he said, "today they're down for ten. Couple times it's twenty."

"There'll be some disappointed faces tomorrow," I said.

He leaned across the bar and tapped my chest with two fingers. "Not for the house, Baby. The house never loses."

He was thinking of his cut. I was thinking of Marty, waiting for me at the end of the line.

"You wanna beer?" he asked.

Breath mints might not have killed the smell of stale sausage, but they wouldn't have hurt.

"Onna house," he said. "Tonight I can afford it."

"Rain check," I said. "I've got a lot of ground to cover."

It was the same story, location after location. Smug grins. Small time proprietors licking their chops. Thinking about their percentage.

The old grocer gave me a relieved smile when I walked into the store.

"I'm glad you finally come," he said. "This much money, it makes Mama afraid. She don't want to come downstairs until you take it away."

Same old story. You got a war to fight, draft some kid who had to leave school awhile to earn next semester's tuition. You got money to move, let some gimp take the risk.

Each stop left me a little more scared than the last. The bigger the load got, the more grief I'd be in for if I lost it.

Lonnie's was lit up like usual. Cars overflowed the lot out along the curb. There was a maroon DeSoto a little way down. Three or four years old. One of the big eight-passenger models they didn't make any more. I recognized it from Fletcher's garage.

I thought about running. Just punch the accelerator. Get the hell out of there. I had a head start. The Ford was new. It had speed. It could out-corner practically anything on the road.

Yeah. Sure.

I could run, but where would I go to hide? LA was home. It was where I longed to come back to all those nights shivering in Korea. I didn't have any place else.

There was nothing I could do but pull around back like I always did.

It was more than just quiet when I got out of the car. It was dead still. No sign of life. Not even stray cats prowling the garbage. That worried me. They were always there. The cats, I mean. Every night. I locked up the Ford and didn't leave the keys.

I didn't dare take the Colt. Any bulge, anything different, someone was bound to notice. Everything had to look just like it always looked.

Lonnie's guy was still counting the take.

"Damn big drop," he drawled without bothering to look at me. "Gonna take me jes' a li'l mo' time heah to tote it all up."

"It's okay." I could hear the jitters in my voice. "I got to make a pit stop."

I went to the john to pull myself together so he wouldn't see me shaking.

The pick-up was normal. Out past the same faceless bowling alley crowd. The same noises. The same smells. It was the creepy kind of normal I remembered coming back from Korea. American soldiers were dying every day and nobody in America acted like anything was unusual. If it didn't touch them personally, they didn't give a rat's ass.

When the service door closed behind me I could feel the hairs on the back of my neck. I was alone, with no idea who might be watching me. I locked the bag in the trunk with the rest and went around to the driver's door, conscious of every step.

Not too fast. Not too slow. Whatever happened, this had to look like just another regular stop on just another regular night.

Nothing happened.

I just got behind the wheel and locked myself in. It was that easy. I started up and pulled around the building, just like usual.

The DeSoto was gone from the front. It wasn't at the garage when I got there. Nothing else was different.

Except me.

I kept my jacket on so nobody would get a look at the sweat stains in the armpits of my shirt.

vi

She was waiting when I got home. Not on the sofa this time. She stood in a corner with her coat buttoned and pointed an automatic at me.

"Shut the door," she said.

I shut the door.

"Move away from it," she said.

I moved away.

"You ratted us," she said.

I shook my head.

"I was there," she said. "In that stupid bowling alley café. Watching."

"To make sure Marty didn't chicken out on you?"

"Sometimes he forgets. Little things. Big things. He just forgets. That's all."

"My mistake."

"They took him," she said. "I saw them put him in a big car and drive off. You ratted us and they took him."

"If I had ratted, they would have taken you too." My voice sounded thick, far off, not very convincing.

"How did they know, then?"

"Marty followed me, didn't he? On the route, I mean. That's how you knew the bowling alley was my last stop."

"So?"

"Fletcher has eyes all over town. People who know every car and every face in every neighborhood." Tomorrow someone would be wearing shiny new Florsheims. Maybe some nice argyles to go with them.

"What will they do to him?" she asked. "Marty?"

"I don't know. What they usually do, I guess. Take him up in the canyons. Screw a gun in his ear."

Her face lost some color.

"It used to be good," she said. "We had plans."

"Yeah," I said.

"It's not so good now. Marty can't hold a job. He got hit in the head too many times. He just can't focus."

"Yeah."

"I had to hock my wedding set to pay the rent."

"I'm sorry."

Her expression soured. "Is this where I hear the big pitch? You're going to take over. Make it right."

I shook my head. "If Fletcher ever connects the two of us, we'll both be joining Marty."

I would go on breathing only as long as Fletcher's guys believed I was just a dumb bag man who had no idea he'd been targeted for a stick-up.

She laughed, a single cold syllable. "Real man, aren't you?"

"I bet on Fletcher. You bet on Marty. One of us had to lose."

"Fletcher made plenty covering bets on Marty's fights. More than Marty was ever paid. He owes us."

Like I was owed for the leg. I helped save the world from the Commies. The VA denied my disability claim.

"If you say so," I said.

She looked at the automatic in her hand. It wasn't going to do her any good now. She put it in her pocket.

"He was, you know," she said.

I didn't say anything. She went to the door and opened it.

"Marty," she said. "He was a real man."

It wasn't much of an epitaph.

She stepped out and closed the door. I never saw her again.

END

Cold War

i

Harv didn't need a newspaper to tell him 1958 was a recession year. He'd had two fares all evening. A couple of sailors headed uptown on a toot and a radio dispatch. He'd found a woman with a battered suitcase and two scared kids on the sidewalk in front of the address. Her husband threw a beer bottle at Harv's taxi, but he was too drunk to hit anything. That's how it was in Siberia.

Okay, so Harv wasn't actually in Siberia. The neighborhood had everything the real article had, except communists. According to the paper they were liable to show up any day if America didn't win the Cold War.

Tonight Siberia was empty of everything but drifting mist and the monotonous cadence of the fog horn in the harbor. Traffic from the harbor was the only reason to have a hack stand in Siberia.

The pedestrian gate in the harbor fence was mounted on a heavy spring. It made a tortured squeak when someone pushed it open. Harv lowered the newspaper for a look.

A man stepped out on the sidewalk. Light from the street lamp was enough to give him his bearings. He headed toward Harv and the taxi.

The man was compact and, judging from his movements, no longer young. He didn't struggle with his suitcase, but he had to adjust his gait to accommodate its weight. Harv folded the paper and rolled down the passenger window.

"This is taxicab?" the man asked.

His accent was foreign, so Harv gave him a pass on the dumb question. "Where to, Mac?"

"You know where is this place?"

He handed a slip of paper through the window. The words *Hotel Madison* were penciled neatly.

"Hop in," Harv said.

The cold engine coughed reluctantly to a semblance of life. The cab was a two year old Studebaker with enough mileage to qualify for a quickie paint job and a sale to some sucker who thought a cheap price and a good deal were the same thing. Harv radioed the destination to dispatch and pulled away from the curb.

It was dark in the rear of the taxi and the passenger's face was lost in the shadows of a turned-up overcoat collar and the brim of a fedora. One arm rested protectively on the suitcase on the seat beside him. The suitcase was leather, and looked expensive. A white silk scarf showed in the vee of the man's overcoat. A foreigner with money.

"Take 'em for a ride," the Dispatcher advised all the drivers. "Put a few extra miles on the meter. They don't know the city. They'll never know the difference."

That wasn't for Harv. His picture and his name were on the hack license displayed by law in the back of the cab. He wanted to keep them clean.

"I didn't know there was any passenger boats due in," Harv said.

"I am sorry," the man replied. "I know you try only to be cordial. I am tired. I do not wish conversation."

There was $4.79 on the meter when Harv pulled up in front of the Madison. The man offered a five dollar bill.

"Is enough?" he asked.

That left Harv a twenty one cent tip. Four point three eight percent of the fare.

Harv had always been quick with numbers. They fascinated him. He had dreamed about college, but he knew he could never scrape together enough money to go.

"Thanks," he said, and took the five.

The man lugged his bag through the lobby door and vanished inside.

The Madison was a budget hotel. Decent, but not the kind of place where the real money stayed.

Harv didn't give it much thought. When you'd driven a hack for a while, nothing surprised you.

He had forgotten all about it when he received the Code 4 dispatch the next night. Code 4 meant driver requested by name. The address was the Madison Hotel.

ii

Fog had turned to drizzle when Harv got to the Madison. The foreigner was waiting under the awning. He must have gotten Harv's name from the hack license displayed in the cab. The question was why he had picked Harv. Any hackie in town would have ridden him wherever he wanted to go.

The light under the awning gave Harv his first good look at the Foreigner's face. Delicate bones, pale skin and wire-rimmed spectacles. The prim face of a school teacher. Or a book keeper. Not someone who kept company with a drop dead gorgeous brunette.

Every town had dames for hire by the evening, weekend or hour, but this honey didn't look like one of them. Her posture was perfect, like maybe she had modeling training. Harv lost interest in the foreigner.

The Brunette's hair was styled to frame a cameo face. Tailoring gave her woolen coat more class than fur could have. It left everything but nylon shaded calves and black patent leather heels to the imagination.

The Foreigner put up an umbrella and escorted her to the cab. A subtle fragrance got in with her. Harv wondered if she knew she was sitting where two years worth of drunks had pissed their pants.

The Foreigner folded down his umbrella and got in beside her. He kept a respectful distance.

"I require transportation for business that must remain private," he told Harv. "Last night you were good enough to refrain from asking questions. I must ask that you render me the same courtesy tonight."

That sounded fishy. Usually fares waited until Harv got talky before they told him to zip it. Okay. So what? That didn't make it a big deal.

Maybe the Brunette was playing hooky. Even the high class dames went looking to get their kicks.

Cab company policy was kiss up to Code 4 fares. Building a book of business they called it. It was either that or Harv could go back to Siberia and listen to the fog horn.

"There's always one question," he said.

"Yes?" the foreigner snapped.

"Where to?"

iii

The *Green Cat* was on Hudson Street, in Chinatown. Every hackie in town had heard about it. A basement nightclub where your fares could find what they couldn't find anywhere else. Neon in the outline of an angry feline cast sinister light on Harv's two passengers as they descended from the sidewalk to the entrance.

The neighborhood gave Harv the willies. It was alien. Claustrophobic. Oriental pictographs took the place of English signs on the fronts of shops shoehorned shoulder to shoulder on the ground floors of tenements that rose into a low overcast.

The faces passing under the street lamp were Asian. Few of them looked friendly. The bits of murmured gibberish that filtered in through the no-draft vent were unintelligible. Harv made sure the doors were locked.

The Eisenhower recession hadn't reached the *Green Cat.* Customers arrived regularly. There was nothing convivial in their manner. They were too well dressed for the neighborhood and they went quickly down the stairs and into the club.

The taxi windows had started to fog by the time Harv's fares came out. The Foreigner had a brown leather case under one arm, pinched tight against his side so he could use both hands to open his umbrella.

"Five thousand American dollars is an artificial number," the Foreigner was saying as the two of them got in. "No expense tally works out to exactly that. We should have insisted on an itemized invoice."

"It amounts to no more than one percent of one percent of the ultimate value of the enterprise," the Brunette responded.

Harv's mental calculator went into gear. That meant something was worth at least fifty million dollars. It sounded like an impossibly large number, but the Brunette had spoken with an authoritative calm that left no doubt it was real. Harv cranked the engine to life and gave the wipers a couple of swipes to clear the windshield.

A man in a raincoat had come out of the *Green Cat* a minute or so after his fares. Now he loitered on the sidewalk. He wasn't looking at the cab. Maybe he really had just paused to light a cigarette.

"Where to?" Harv asked.

iv

Harv knew the town inside out, but he had never heard of Ocean View Drive. The number 12711 was too big to fit inside the city limits.

"Where's that," he asked.

"Take the Coast Highway south," the Brunette instructed. "I'll tell you when to turn."

Harv radioed the destination to dispatch.

The Coast Highway snaked its way out of the city. Traffic thinned and the lights of the suburbs up on the flanking hills grew fewer and farther apart.

"Next turn on the left," the Brunette instructed.

Fresh asphalt curled up into the hills and ended at the beginnings of a development. Streets were laid out and the skeletons of a few houses under construction were visible in the headlights. Only one had been finished. A lighted sign identified it as a model home.

"Stop here," the Brunette instructed.

The model home was dark inside. A black Lincoln sedan filled the driveway. The car had Consular license plates. It was empty, and it had been parked long enough to collect a light coat of drizzle.

"If any car approaches, honk your horn," the Foreigner said.

He and the Brunette got out. The model home swallowed the two of them as if they had never existed. Harv was alone again.

Harv was born and raised in the city. Bright lights and clamor and nonstop movement. The stillness of the hills made him edgy. The occasional chirp of a cricket grated on his nerves. The only sign of civilized life was the steady flash of the airport beacon miles to the south, reflecting off the bases of low clouds.

An hour dragged by before his fares returned.

"I hope you were not taken in by the fellow's courtly manner," the Foreigner was saying. "He knew exactly the right questions to slip into the conversation."

"Shrewd men often rise in life by playing the fool," the Brunette responded. "As long as they are led to believe their pretense is succeeding, they will remain docile. If they sense that it is failing, they can become dangerous."

It sounded like a good time to get away from there. Harv cranked life out of the old Studebaker before any demons could find their way out of the dark house.

"Where to?" he asked.

v

The Turnbury Building was no longer the tallest skyscraper in the city, but it was still a prestige address. Hackies avoided it whenever they could. The stuffed shirt lawyers and investment bankers who charged fat fees in the offices there were notorious for stingy tips. Harv waited while his two fares went in.

The city was catnapping through the quiet hours between the time the restaurants closed and the theaters let out. The sidewalk was empty and only a few cars drifted past under the street lamps. Harv retrieved his newspaper from under the seat.

There was an article about jet airliners flying passengers non-stop to and from Europe at six hundred miles an hour. Big deal. They still needed a smelly old taxi to get them through the traffic jam to their fancy hotel. Harv put the paper away.

His fares were back.

"I never cease to be astonished," the Foreigner was saying as they got in, "at the level of arrogance these people can muster."

"If you thought they were obnoxious tonight, you should hear them after they've had a few cocktails," the Brunette said. "The important thing is the agreements are signed and the money can start flowing."

The Foreigner held up a warning hand. "Driver, you will take us please back to the hotel."

"Sure thing," Harv said.

Okay, so the guy didn't want some hackie overhearing his secrets. That was just fine. This business didn't sound like it was completely on the level anyway. What Harv didn't know couldn't hurt him. He started up and pulled away from the curb.

A Chevrolet came out of nowhere and cut him off. He slammed on the brakes and the old Studebaker slewed to a jolting stop. Before he could sound an angry blast on the horn another car screeched to a stop immediately behind. High beams threw blinding light into the taxi.

Red emergency lights began pulsing on the rear passenger shelf of the Chevrolet. Men in raincoats piled out of both cars. Two had carbines. The others brandished revolvers. One of them rapped a badge against Harv's window.

"FBI. Shut off the engine."

vi

The FBI Agent repeated himself until Harv pried his wits loose from the grip of terror and reached for the ignition key. All four doors of the taxi were pulled open.

"Everyone out. Keep your hand in sight. Make no sudden moves."

Harv climbed out gingerly, with his hands in front of him, squinting against the headlight beams shining through the cab. The soles of his shoes slithered on the damp pavement and threatened to upset him. An agent grabbed the shoulder of his jacket, shoved him against the front fender of the cab and told him to put his hands flat on the hood.

Harv's eyes began to adjust to the glare. He could make out the

Foreigner on his side of the taxi with his hands flat on the trunk lid. The Brunette was on the other side in the same position.

The two agents with carbines stood guard. The others had put their revolvers away. One searched Harv. Two others were searching his fares. The syncopated flash of red emergency lights gave everything the hellish aura of a nightmare.

One of the agents seemed to be in charge. "Get me IDs on these people."

He collected them, settled into the front seat of the Chevrolet and lifted a radiotelephone handset from the dashboard.

The agent guarding Harv said: "Stand up. Put your hands behind your back."

The handcuffs were cold when they snapped over Harv's wrists. A brisk wind blew chilling drizzle into his face. Nothing was going right, just from bad to worse.

The Agent in Charge finished his call and strode to where the Foreigner stood handcuffed. He thumbed through the pages of a passport.

"I don't see anything here that shows you entered the country legally. Do you have any documentation that shows you cleared customs?"

"I am sorry," the Foreigner said. "I do not wish conversation."

His voice was quiet, polite, unafraid.

The agent guarding the Foreigner displayed an automatic pistol held by a pencil inserted into the barrel.

"Maybe he does his talking with this."

The Agent in Charge retrieved the Foreigner's leather case from the rear seat of the cab.

"You picked this up at the *Green Cat*."

Harv remembered the man in the raincoat who had come out of the nightclub right after the Foreigner and the Brunette. He had the same *London Fog* look as the two car loads of agents.

Standing handcuffed in the drizzle hadn't seemed to bother the Brunette. She had stiffened only when the Agent in Charge retrieved the leather case.

"Do you have a warrant?" she asked.

The Agent in charge ignored her, settled in the rear of the taxi and opened the case. He removed sheaves of blue-backed paperwork. Time stood still while he inspected them page by page. Drizzle accumulated in Harv's hair. It began to drip down the back of his neck before the Agent in Charge finally finished and climbed out of the taxi.

"The CIA and the State Department are going to have a field day with this," he told the Foreigner.

Silence.

"You went south, toward the airport," the Agent in Charge told the Foreigner. "Did you meet someone who had entered the country illegally by plane?"

Harv's stomach turned queasy. They were spies. He had been riding a couple of spies around. It was easy to guess how the FBI knew the route he had taken. They didn't need to follow him. They picked up his hack number outside the *Green Cat* and called the cab company. Harv had radioed every destination to dispatch.

"Look, Mister," he said to the agent guarding him, "I'm just a hackie. I don't know these people. I don't know what they're doing or nothing like that. I just ride people around. They tell me where to go and I ride them there. I don't know them. I don't know nothing about them."

That sounded good, until Harv remembered this was a Code 4 dispatch. The Foreigner had requested him by name.

"We'll have a nice long talk about that," the Agent promised.

"Radio call," someone said to the Agent in Charge.

He took the leather case over to the Chevrolet and got in.

Harv began shivering. He was going to prison. His name would be in all the papers. Everyone who ever knew him would think he was a traitor to the country.

The Agent in Charge climbed out of the Chevrolet. His movements were slow, reluctant.

"We won't be needing these people tonight," he announced. "Remove the handcuffs and return everything."

Just like that. No explanation. No apology, like maybe they had made a mistake.

Harv knew better than to ask questions. He didn't get many good breaks in life. When they came he knew to keep his mouth shut and count his blessings. He fumbled his possessions back into his pockets.

The car that came for the Brunette wasn't just any Cadillac. It was the latest model limousine, as shiny as if it had just been driven off the showroom floor. A chauffeur in a gray uniform held an umbrella while he escorted her. It didn't matter that she was already sodden from half an hour in the drizzle. The guy was a chauffeur, and that's what chauffeurs did.

The Cadillac rolled away and the tail lights vanished into the mist.

The agents got back in their Chevrolets, turned off the emergency lights and drove away. Harv and the Foreigner were left standing in the drizzle. Harv blocked the Foreigner from getting into the cab.

"Are you some kind of communist?"

Harv was an American. Pistol or no pistol, he wasn't riding any commies.

"Do you think your FBI would have release me if I were communist?" the Foreigner asked.

"I don't get that. I don't get none of it."

"I will explain on the way back to the hotel," the Foreigner said. "You may not like it, but I will explain."

vii

The Foreigner got in, took off his spectacles and began cleaning the lenses with a handkerchief.

"You know of the Cold War."

"I heard of it," Harv said, and pulled into traffic.

"You see television and you read the newspapers and you ask me if I am communist. If you drove a taxi in Petrograd, you would ask if I am capitalist lackey. In Shanghai, if I am running dog imperialist."

"That's commie talk," Harv said.

"It is camouflage. It permits nations to be ruled by a privileged few who have amassed wealth and power far beyond their numbers."

The Foreigner hooked his spectacles over his ears.

"Taxicab drivers are indoctrinated with the need to be patriotic. So they will not dare to ask why they cannot be the ones to attend fine universities and develop their talents."

It was like the guy could look into Harv's soul. "What does that have to do with what happened tonight?"

"Do you think the wealthy and powerful would prefer to defeat the enemies of their nation or to amass more wealth and power for themselves?"

"Why ask me? I'm just a hackie."

"Enterprise requires agreements to obtain raw materials, recruit technical expertise, arrange shipping and raise investment capital. Such cooperation may infringe upon laws enacted to prosecute the Cold War. The agreements must be put in place without drawing attention to the enterprise."

"Yeah?" Harv said, and brought the cab to a stop in front of the Madison.

"You will wait while I retrieve my luggage and discharge my obligation to the hotel."

Harv was ready when the Foreigner came out.   "You didn't say about the FBI."

"They have sources of information. They investigate suspicious activity. Sometimes they learn things they are not meant to know."

"They just walked away," Harv said.

"It is not as you have seen in the cinema. They answer to superior authority that is appointed by and answers to the wealthy and the powerful."

"So it's like the golden rule?" Harv asked. "Whoever has the gold makes the rules?"

"The American idiom may not be the most eloquent, but it is by far the most colorful."

The Foreigner paid his fare with crisp twenties. Harv's tip worked out to $4.79. The Foreigner took his suitcase and disappeared through the pedestrian gate to board a boat he had never left and leave a country where he had never been.

The foghorn gave Harv the succulent razzberry, and kept rubbing it in.

Okay, so maybe he was just Harv the hackie. Maybe all he would ever be good for was holding down a shift in Siberia. The big shots still had to climb into his smelly old Studebaker and sit where two years worth of drunks had pissed their pants if they wanted to get where they were going.

END

Protection Racket

Rollo stopped on the sidewalk outside a haberdasher's shop. It was evening and the shop was closed. The display window was dark enough for him to size up his reflection. Black shirt. White tie. Collar bar with little diamonds at each end. Solid class. He drew himself up to his full five feet seven inches and strode confidently to the little grocery store on the corner.

Nothing had changed. The familiar bell announced his arrival when he opened the door. He looked down the same aisles he had swept out when he came to help after school. The memory brought a smile. The shelves he had stocked when he got a little older were the same, nicked and worn by years of shoppers but clean and replenished for the next customers. He ran a finger over the old cash register that had stood at the end of the counter for as long as he could remember.

The old man came from the back looking the same in his white grocer's apron. Passing years had left his gray hair thinner. The stoop of arthritis was a little more obvious. There were no customers at that time of the evening, but he still managed to walk with the expectant spring in his step that Rollo remembered.

"Hi, Pop."

"Rollo, my boy."

The old man took him by both arms and looked him up and down. The appraisal was a wordless criticism. Okay. So what if he wasn't impressed by the way Rollo dressed? This was a small town. An old town. People here just didn't get it.

"How's everything?" Rollo asked.

"You would not need to ask," the old man said, "if you came home to stay instead of just visiting."

It was the same thing Rollo had heard a hundred times, but it still made him squirm.

"Come on, Pop, you know this ain't for me."

"What isn't?"

"This kind of living. The store and all. I was never no good doin' numbers in school. Never no good wit' the customers."

"What are you good with?" The old man worried at what he saw on Rollo's face.   "The band-aid over your eye. What is that?"

"Little cut. Don't mean nothin'. It'll heal up. They always do."

The old man had something to say about that, but movement outside the front window caught his eye and stopped him. The color left his face. He released Rollo's arms.

Rollo glanced out.

A white convertible had pulled up and parked at the curb. A shiny new nineteen sixty one Ford. There were two men in the front seat.

"What's the matter, Pop?" Rollo asked. "Those guys giving you problems?"

"It is nothing," the old man said. "Just a little business."

His words were nervous, and came out too quickly. He tried to hurry around the counter to the cash register, but Rollo stepped in his way and stopped him.

"Are they shakin' you down?"

"What does that mean?"

"Are they making you pay so they don't cause no trouble? So they don't beat you up? So they don't wreck the store?"

"It's a matter of a little money to stop a lot of trouble."

"You ain't got money for that, Pop."

"Please don't interfere."

"You don't hardly make no money off this place," Rollo said.

"I know you mean well, but this is for me to decide."

"You're a sucker for anyone in the neighborhood havin' a hard time."

"I will take care of this and then we will talk, you and me."

The bell sounded a warning note when the first man pushed in through the door. He was good looking in a meaty sort of way, six inches taller than Rollo and at least fifty pounds heavier. The hick town version of a sharp dresser. Pleated trousers and shiny shoes. His shirt had cost money. Glossy fabric with a turned up collar and a design in black and cream that did its best to make him look even bigger than he was.

His expression was smug, but his eyes darted swiftly, checking to see if there were people down the aisles. Looking for anyone or anything that might mean trouble for him.

The man who drifted in casually behind him was an inch shorter and a few pounds trimmer. His facial features were perfect, like a model on the cover of a magazine. Slicked back hair, trimmed exactly at the sideburns. His tailored sport coat had too much class for the neighborhood. Too much class for the guy wearing it.

A beefcake and a pretty boy. Vultures feeding off honest people who couldn't fight back. Taking hard earned money from an old man so they could dress up nice and ride around in a fancy car.

"Okay, Grandpa," Pretty Boy said, "get it up. We ain't got all night."

The old man started for the register, shuffling helplessly, resigned and resentful. Rollo got in his way again and wouldn't move.

"Forget it, Pop. You don't have to pay creeps like these."

Beefcake stared in disbelief at the insolence. He had to think about it for a minute before he decided to let out a mocking laugh.

"Hey, Grandpa," he said, looking down at Rollo. "Where did you get the midget?"

Rollo wasn't amused and he wasn't impressed. "Get lost, why don'tcha?"

"Why don't you?" Beefcake shot back. "Before someone steps on you."

He moved a couple of steps closer and loomed over Rollo.

"No," the old man said. "No trouble. It is not necessary. I will pay."

Rollo wasn't having any of it. He poked a left jab into Beefcake's nose.

The punch drew blood and fury. Rollo danced away from an angry roundhouse, stepped in and whipped a right cross into the side of Beefcake's head.

The blow was delivered with professional snap and precision. Beefcake took a couple of stumbling steps and couldn't get his balance. He bumped a display of soup cans going down on one knee. He looked dazed and confused. The display threatened to topple over on him.

Pretty Boy moved in fast. He came straight at Rollo. He was all speed and no finesse, and caught a left for his efforts.

Rollo danced away from Pretty Boy's return punch and kept dancing, moving in and out, delivering sharp, precise jabs.

Pretty Boy did his best to keep his guard up and land his own punches, but he lacked Rollo's speed, grace and coordination.

Rollo seemed to have eyes in the back of his head. He danced backward, weaving one way and then the other. Up on the balls of his feet, deftly avoiding the counter and displays

Rollo's blood was up and he was having fun. He concentrated on Pretty Boy's face, the eyes and mouth, jabbing and retreating and moving in to strike again. Spoiler shots that Pretty Boy would still see in the mirror way into next month.

The old man saw them and shuddered. He had lived a life of peace, and had taken every opportunity to encourage Rollo to do the same. He watched his dreams evaporate in a flurry of violence.

Beefcake was back on his feet. He had regained his balance. He tested his movement. The eyes that lurked behind pads of flesh above his cheeks were small and shrewd and mean.

"Get behind the shrimp," he told Pretty Boy. "Grab his arms. Hold his still. I'm going to teach him a lesson he'll never forget."

Pretty Boy tried, but he wasn't up to the task. His legs were wobbly and slow to respond. He squinted like he was having trouble seeing out of one eye.

Beefcake came anyway, pumping his arms like pistons, down low to deliver devastating body blows.

It was a sucker move that left him wide open for a head shot. Rollo danced out of harm's way and moved in fast to deliver a combination.

Beefcake stumbled sideways. He was able to keep his footing, but that was all. His face was a mask of confusion. Blood ran from his nose, dripped off his jaw and dribbled down the front of his fancy shirt. He looked around for help.

Pretty Boy had retreated the door. The fight had gone out of him. He put a hand to his mouth and brought it away with a bloody tooth between his fingers. He stared at the tooth in dismay.

Beefcake made his way to the door. He kept a wary eye on Rollo.

Rollo hopped from one foot to the other. His arms hung loose at his sides, ready for more if the pair were foolish enough to challenge him.

"Get lost," he said. "The both of you."

They made their way out the door, beaten and bewildered. Defeat was a new experience for them. They didn't seem to know how to deal with it.

"And stay lost," Rollo called after them. "Don't make me come back."

Rollo was skipping rope in the gym, watching a sparring match in the ring and waiting for a turn on the speed bag when Art came out of the office. Art was bald and thickset, with a hammered down look. Black chest hair curled out at the open collar of a breakfast-stained shirt. He didn't have Rollo's grace, and he didn't need it. When Art moved, people got out of his way. That was the kind of connections he had.

"So, Rollo," he said in his hoarse rumble, "you finally come back to the big town."

"What's wit' finally?" Rollo asked. "I'm only gone two days."

"So how are things out in the sticks?"

"I went to see my old man. He's got this little grocery store. Nothin' big, but he spent his life building it up. I remember the hours he worked. The nights he worried over the books. I get there and what do I find? Two guys shakin' him down."

"What guys?"

"I dunno. Just guys."

"Were they connected?"

"Nah."

"How do you know?"

Art had big, staring eyes, like a toad. They told you when he wanted a straight answer and wanted it right quick. Rollo quit jumping rope.

"They was all size, no class," he said. "No footwork. No hand speed. All they done was waddle around and take head shots. Nobody wit' connections would use no stumblebums like that."

"Yeah?" Art's rumble was as close to satisfied as he ever got. "Well, this ain't no rest home. Here's a list of merchants that ain't paid up this week. Climb into your street clothes and get to work."

END

Dead Reckoning

Ernie was parking cars in Vegas that November. The November President Kennedy was killed. At a little place off the Strip. Valet parkers on the Strip got fancy jackets. Ernie got a chintzy vest. He couldn't wear anything over it that might cover the club logo. November nights were cold in the desert. Ernie was jitterbugging to keep warm when Red Maserati came out.

Ernie never knew their names. Only their cars. This was a car you wouldn't forget. The only Maserati Ernie had ever driven. Almost brand new. Just running it back to the lot gave him a rush. Blipping the throttle and listening to the throaty exhaust.

The guy who owned it was broad and bulky. A white sport coat made him look even wider than he was. Black chest air curled up in the open collar of a pink shirt. His slacks were black and his loafers were black patent leather with white tassels. He was stewed to the gills.

"Gimme my car," he ordered.

"I'd like to," Ernie said, "only I can't"

Liquor left the big man wordless, confused.

"They got this policy," Ernie explained. "The Management. If a guy's had too much to drink, I can't give him his car keys."

The big man's face got flushed and mean.

"It ain't my fault," Ernie said. "It's the policy. The Management, they'd fire me if I--"

Red Maserati balled a hairy hand into fist. The punch was a drunken roundhouse that that gave Ernie time to jitterbug backwards. The punch missed and the big man lost his balance. He went down in a heap.

That was when Gray Oldsmobile came out. They were a couple in their fifties. The guy was a business type, quietly dressed, except for a gaudy tie. His wife probably made him wear it. She was tall and bony. A pinched face gave her a permanent look of grim determination. They both looked down at the big man.

"Too much to drink," Ernie said.

"Loudmouth lush," the man said. "Inside popping off about how he knew who killed Kennedy. They should've thrown him out an hour ago."

That sounded odd. The Management didn't like disturbances. When a drunk got loud Al, the big greeter, would show him the door right quick.

Ernie went back and brought the Oldsmobile up. The man held door for his wife.

"It's a mourning period," he was saying. "Kennedy was President. They need to have a mourning period."

"So he was President," she snapped back. "That doesn't mean they have to ruin everyone's Thanksgiving. I was really looking forward to seeing the grandchildren. Now I'll have to wait for Christmas."

Her husband closed her into the car, came around and drove off. No tip.

"Yeah, sure," Ernie said. "Your old lady rags you so you take it out on the car parker. Screw you."

Red Maserati was back on his feet. He was shuffling a little, still trying to establish his balance.

"I heard what he said. Loudmouth lush, he called me."

"There's a motel across the street," Ernie said.

"I was there when they planned it. The whole Kennedy thing. I was there and I heard them planning it."

"Maybe you could get a room for the night," Ernie suggested. "Kind of sleep it off."

"You know what the big deal was? Fixing the motorcade route. Getting Kennedy close to a building where the windows opened. Most of the buildings today, they're air conditioned and the windows don't open. That and getting his car slowed down enough so their guy could shoot him."

"Your car will be safe here," Ernie assured him. "We'll take real good care of it."

"You know how they pulled that off?" the big man asked. "Juice. Right up to the top."

"Why don't you kind of go on up to the crosswalk," Ernie suggested.

"I was there. I heard them planning it. I used to be somebody. Once. I used to get respect."

"Wait until the light changes your way," Ernie said. "Then go on over to the motel."

The big man had recovered some balance. He was getting sore. Ernie got ready to jitterbug, but he wasn't sore at Ernie. He was sore at the world. He turned unsteadily until he was facing the street.

"I used to get respect," he began bellowing over and over at the thin traffic drifting by.

White Cadillac came out before Ernie could think of a way to quiet him down. She had been a looker once. Maybe a dancer. She came in occasionally, always alone. She always left with a younger guy. She handed Ernie her chit with a dollar bill folded around it, like always. Like a single was a big tip. Maybe it was when your Cadillac was four years old.

The car had been class once. Now it had a piece of tape where the convertible top was ripped and a spider web crack at the corner of the windshield. Ernie brought it to a stop under the port-cochere.

"I saw Kennedy once, right here in Vegas," White Cadillac was saying to the young guy with her. "Before he was President. He was so close I could of reached out and touched him."

"Why would you want to do that?" the guy asked.

"Do what?"

"Reach out and touch Kennedy back when he was nobody?"

"I didn't say I wanted to. I just said he was so close I could of. That's all I said."

White Cadillac and her one night stand got into the car and she pulled out onto the street. Her tail lights vanished into the night.

Red Maserati had run out of steam. He was weaving his way up toward the intersection and the crosswalk that would take him to the motel.

It was a slow night. Probably because of the Kennedy thing. Ernie went back to jitterbugging, doing his best to stay warm.

He never saw the hit and run.

He heard the ugly thump. When he looked Red Maserati was lying the in the street. An inert lump in the crosswalk. The tail lights of a pick-up truck were receding into the distance, too far for him to see anything. He hot-footed to the door and shoved it open.

"Call the cops," he yelled in at Al, the greeter. "A guy just got run down in the street."

"Forget it," Al said. "The Management wants no trouble."

"But he's lying out there."

"Forget it. Let somebody else call. Just go back to your job."

The automatic closer pushed the door back in Ernie's face. He heard a siren in the distance. Someone must have already called. Everything would be all right. Well, maybe not all right, but there was nothing he could do about it.

Cop cars and an ambulance came. Ernie watched them load Red Maserati onto a wheeled stretcher and drape a sheet over him. He was dead because Ernie wouldn't give him his car keys. Dead because Ernie sent him to the motel instead.

A guy in a suit came from the intersection. He was heavyset, with a lot of weight in his shoulders and even more around his midsection. He came with a slow, deliberate waddle and showed Ernie a badge.

"Did you see the accident?"

Ernie caught a scent of liquor on the cop's breath.

"No, Officer."

"You don't call me officer. Someone in uniform talks to you, you call him officer. I'm a detective. You call me detective."

"Yes, sir. Yes, Detective."

"You were standing right here. How come you didn't see the accident?"

"I wasn't looking. It's a quiet street. Nothing ever happens there."

"Did you know the victim?"

"No, sir. No, Detective. I mean, he came here a few times. I only saw him because I park the cars here."

"He have a car here?"

"Yes, sir. Yes, Detective."

"Keys."

The detective snapped his fingers and held out a meaty hand, palm up. Ernie went and got them. The detective bounced them in his hand.

"If he had a car, how come he was walking?"

"I wouldn't give him the keys," Ernie said. "I mean I couldn't. He had too much to drink. That's the policy. If they had too much to drink, I can't give them the keys."

The detective thought about it for a minute. He looked at the club and then at the intersection and then across at the motel and then down the street in the direction the truck must have come from. Not so much looking as measuring and considering.

"So he gets sloshed in the club. You won't give him the keys, so all he can do is cross the street to the motel. Is that it?"

"It wasn't my fault," Ernie said. "It's the policy."

"Slick," the detective said. "He say anything to you?"

Ernie felt a chill run up his spine. Red Maserati had been shooting his mouth off about Kennedy. About knowing how he got killed. Ernie didn't want any part of that.

"Just he wanted his keys."

"That's all?"

"He was yelling at cars on the street."

"About what?"

"I don't know. He was drunk. He was yelling something about respect."

The detective stood close to Ernie, looming over him and studying him with small eyes narrowed by pads of fat. It was an effort not to squirm.

"Okay," the detective finally said. "Here's how it is. You did your duty. You talked to the police. You don't talk to anyone else about this. Ever. Got that?"

"Yeah, sure," Ernie blurted. "I mean, yes, Detective."

The cop pocketed the keys to the Maserati and waddled off. Ernie watched him all the way out of sight before he started breathing normally again. He went back to jitterbugging, but it didn't help. The kind of chill he felt went all the way down to his bones.

Red Maserati really had been somebody once. He must have been, or he wouldn't have had the money to buy the car. The Management hadn't thrown him out when he started talking about how Kennedy was shot.

Loudmouth drunks never lasted more than five minutes without getting the boot.

"Slick," the detective had said,

Like he knew it had all been planned. Like someone had kept Red Maserati in the club until he got good and drunk. Someone who knew Ernie would send him across the street, where the truck was waiting to shut his mouth permanently.

Juice. All the way up to the top. That's what Red Maserati had said. Juice. All the way to the top.

Ernie would never know for sure, but he knew the question would haunt him the rest of his life.

END

Eleven Bush

The restaurant was a grease pit. When you were just back from Vietnam and scraping through college on the GI Bill, you didn't eat with the elite.

I had overheard the place mentioned on campus. After a weekend of stacking crates to pick up a few extra bucks I didn't feel like cooking. I just wanted something cheap to eat while I crammed for tomorrow's mid-term.

The evening crowd looked more drop-out than college. Glassy eyes. No visible energy. Laid back, they called it.

The only empty table was next to a dingy window. I glance-read the menu and decided there wasn't much they could do to fuck up a hot beef sandwich.

Two kids came in and sat down across the table from me. Nineteen, maybe twenty. A guy and a chick. Both keyed up and glancing out the window.

"You mind?" the guy asked.

He was tall, skinny. Shoulder length hair. Tie dyed undershirt. Denim jacket with a peace symbol. The latest edition of Joe College.

"We're waiting for someone," the chick said.

She was a little on the pudgy side. Cotton print dress with too many colors. Stringy hair under a beaded headband. Peace symbol necklace. You weren't college without a peace symbol.

"We're going to score," the guy said.

I went back to my text book.

He didn't like that. They were doing something naughty. He probably thought I should be impressed.

"What are you majoring in?" he asked.

"Business Administration. Accounting."

"You're going to be part of the system?"

He made it sound like a case of leprosy. I didn't see any point in discussing it.

"Chip is majoring in Poli Sci," the chick said.

That was short for Political Science. If you wanted to be cool, you majored in Political Science. For me college was about climbing off the bottom rung of the ladder. Cool was on Chip's agenda, not mine.

"That's an army jacket, isn't it?" Chip asked.

"Yeah." Like it wasn't obvious.

"The Vietnam War is immoral," the chick told me.

"It wasn't my war. I was just eleven bush."

"What?" Chip asked.

Eleven bush was boonie rat slang for military occupational specialty 11B. Light weapons infantryman. It wasn't the sort of thing you understood when you had daddy financing a college draft deferment.

"Cannon fodder," I said.

"What are you going to do when The Revolution comes?" Chip asked.

"Ask me when it gets here," I said.

The Revolution was an article of faith on campus. The hair-heads were going to take over the world. Everyone was going to smoke dope and sing protest songs.

I didn't have to tell the two kids to push off. A van pulled into the gravel parking lot. It stopped out in the shadows, away from the building. The headlights of passing cars showed faded paint and splotches of primer. Someone had sprayed a big peace symbol on the side. Red neon from the restaurant sign gave it a vaguely satanic cast. The kids saw it and stood up.

The chick gave me a worried look. I wasn't conforming to the socially acceptable brand of non-conformism.

"The Revolution is coming," she warned, and the two of them went out.

I spent the next hour working sum-of-the-years-digits depreciation problems while I filled the hole in my stomach.

The chick came back alone. Her dress was rumpled. The color was gone from her face. Her eyes were red. She sat across from me. She stared at nothing and said nothing.

That was fine with me.

A guy came to the table. Mid-twenties. Muscular. Beard. The peace symbol looked out of place on his leather vest.

"Hey," he said to the chick. "Party's outside."

She stared straight ahead and didn't say anything.

"Hey, come on," the guy said. "You're coming with us."

She didn't speak or look at him. In order to make eye contact with her, he would have to be sitting where I was. He pushed my shoulder.

"Hey, man. You're in my seat."

I'd had enough of people pushing into my life.

"Fuck off, Mattress Face."

He grabbed my jacket and tried to haul me out of the chair. He probably thought he was bullying some college boy.

I didn't bother standing. I just lunged out of the chair and drove my shoulder into his hip to knock him off balance. I grabbed his leg and yanked upward to spill him on his head and shoulders. That left the small of his back exposed. I gave him a swift kick in the kidneys.

He tried to squirm away and get to his feet. I didn't know how many times I kicked him in the head. I just knew how good I felt doing it.

When I was done there was a man about a foot in front of me. Maybe three hundred pounds of him. He didn't have much hair. He wasn't wearing a peace symbol. He didn't really need the billy club he was slapping into his palm. His breath was enough to knock over the whole room.

"Okay, pal," he said. "Time to pay up and take it on the arches."

"Yeah," I said. "I hear you."

The fight and the frustration were gone. It happened that way sometimes. The adrenaline came in a rush and then it was gone just as fast. Not often enough to be a problem. Just every once in a while. Like the bad dreams. I collected my textbook and notes and let baldy walk me to the cash register.

Customers righted a few chairs they had spilled avoiding the scuffle and went back to being laid back.

Two more fur-faced toughs came in. They didn't like seeing their buddy on the floor. Baldy went over to console them.

"I don't want trouble in my place," he said. "Get this piece of shit out of here."

"Hey, man, what happened to--," one of them began, and got the business end of the billy club in his stomach.

"That's like right fucking now," Baldy said.

That sounded like my exit line.

Chip was outside, sitting on the bumper of a Volkswagen. At least that's where he was physically. From the look in his eyes, he had left the planet. The chick had him by the arm, shaking him and not having any luck bringing him back to Earth.

I got my car started.

The passenger door opened and the chick got in fast and shut it. The car was an old Valiant. It had been the cheapest thing on the cheapest lot in town. The door locks had never worked.

She sat against the door, as far away from me as she could get without pushing it open and falling out.

"Can you ride me to my dorm?" she asked.

I pushed the Drive button and pulled out onto the two lane. Right now I wanted distance. We could discuss details later.

"They said I wasn't liberated," the chick told me.

I checked the mirror. We didn't seem to have any company.

"You know?" she asked.

"Yeah. I get it. They fed Chip enough junk to keep him quiet and took you in the van and liberated you."

"That's not what liberated means." She tried to snap at me, but it came out more like a sniffle.

"It doesn't mean anything," I said. "It's just a word. Like dedicated."

"Like what?"

"Dedicated. It's a word they used a lot in 'Nam. The platoon lieutenant was always telling us how the country was depending on us to be dedicated."

"Dedicated to what?"

"Nothing. It was just something that came down the chain of command."

"The what?"

"The Generals. The Colonels. The Captains. They didn't have a strategy to win the war. All they could do was tell us to be dedicated."

"What did you tell them?"

"Nothing. Nobody did. So we weren't dedicated. So what could they do to us? Send us to Vietnam?"

"It's McCarthy Hall," she said.

We were getting closer to the campus. There were street lights here, and more traffic. Her features were tense in the growing brightness, and there were nerves in her voice.

"My dorm," she said. "It's McCarthy Hall."

"Yeah. I get it."

I dropped her there. She watched me pull away. I caught a glimpse of her in the mirror, heading for one of the other dorms. She hadn't wanted me to know where she lived.

Her common sense had kicked in a little late. It had probably dawned on her what would follow if she reported what had happened. The police would learn she and Chip were buying drugs. The whole mess would go public. She would be the campus gossip. Her parents would give her no end of grief. She could keep her mouth shut or become a martyr.

She didn't know how lucky she was. When her sophomore larks went to hell, she could bum a ride back to her dorm. In Vietnam, fifteen year old girls were sold into brothels. There was no ride back to the dorm. No dorm to ride back to. Just endless nights of drunken foreigners, drugs and beatings.

Maybe most of them were tough enough to survive. Get out in one piece. Beat the venereal disease. Beat the addiction. Get on with whatever passed for life in a country being torn apart by an endless war.

You couldn't explain that sort of thing to a suburban princess.

It was like the whole war. You couldn't talk to people about it. People who hadn't been there. They hadn't carried fifty pounds of gear and slogged through one meaningless day after another in hundred twenty degree heat. They hadn't been drenched in monsoons. They hadn't loaded what was left of their friends onto med-evac choppers.

They were spectators. To them it was all just flickering images on television. Backdrop for some rock star reporter who had dressed up in a fatigue jacket so he would look like he knew what he was talking about when he told them what to think.

Fuck them. I had survived. I had gotten back to the world in one piece. I had earned the right to flip them off and get on with my own life.

END

Prom Night

Two guys came into the *Nite Spot* and sat on stools at the counter. It was raining outside and they were dripping wet. The older one might have been nineteen.

"I need to see some ID," I said.

They just stared at me. Both of them wore baseball caps. Trench coats made them seem even smaller than they were.

"We serve beer," I told them. "You got to be twenty one to eat here."

They looked around. Except for Bett and me, the *Nite Spot* was empty. Bett was the waitress. On Saturdays she hung around late, hoping to pick up a little extra money. She wasn't much to look at, but she wore tight jeans and when she smiled her acne scars weren't so bad. It was enough for tips, so she hung around and read romance books while she waited for table customers.

"I got to see some ID," I told the two guys again. "It's the law."

"We don't want no trouble," the older one said. "Do we, Robin?"

"No." Robin sounded jumpy.

"No, we don't want no trouble." The older one unbuttoned his trench coat, took out a blue steel automatic and pointed it at me. "You ain't going to give us no trouble, are you?"

"No sir." My mouth was dry. I could hardly talk.

"See what's in the till, Robin."

Robin unbuttoned his trench coat and took out a smaller automatic. He came around behind the counter and opened the register.

"Check under the drawer," the older one said. "The big bills are always under the drawer."

"You told me that a hundred times already, Denny."

Denny poked me with the muzzle of his automatic. "Hand over your wallet."

I put it on the counter. "Not much in it. I don't bring much. We been held up before."

"Is that what you think this is?" Denny asked. "A hold up?"

"Yeah." I looked at his gun, then over at Robin emptying the till. "Sure."

"Well, it ain't."

I wondered what it was, but I was too scared to ask him.

"You know what night this is?" he asked me.

"Saturday."

"It's prom night," he said. "Ain't it, Robin."

"Don't start in on me." Robin's voice was tight, angry.

"Robin didn't go to the prom. Did you, Robin?"

"Not here, Denny. Not in front of them."

Denny ignored him. "You know why not?"

"No," I said.

"His girl went with a nigger."

The *Nite Spot* was very quiet. I could hear the faint buzz of the electric wall clock, and the steady drip of rain outside.

Denny looked over at Bett. "What do you think about that?"

Bett hadn't moved since they came in, except to put down her book. "I don't know," she said, then remembered to smile.

"You work here?" Denny asked.

"Yeah."

"Waitress? Like that?"

"Yeah."

"Make good money, do you?"

She just shrugged.

"Lots of tips?"

"It depends."

"Bring it here."

40

She came over and put a few bills and some coins on the counter. Her smile was stiff, scared.

"What do you think?" Denny asked her.

"About what?"

"About Robin's girl. About her going to the prom with a nigger?"

Robin came around the counter and put down the money from the till. "She ain't my girl."

"You're always looking at her picture in that stupid yearbook."

"I just like her. That's all."

"Maybe she already had a date," Bett suggested. "I mean, when you asked her."

"I never asked her," Robin said.

Denny shoved him. "A man don't ask. He takes."

"Don't push me."

"You ever had any pussy?"

"Just because you're my brother don't mean you can push me."

"You ever even seen pussy?"

"I seen pussy."

"What's it look like?"

Robin fidgeted.

"Well?"

"Like…like pussy."

Denny poked Bett with his automatic. "Take off your pants. Show him your pussy."

She backpedaled. Denny grabbed the front of her blouse. He wasn't much bigger than she was. He had to pull hard to stop her. Half the front of her blouse ripped away in his hand. She stumbled back against a stool and crossed her arms over her exposed bra.

"Hey, guys," I said, "maybe this isn't such a good idea, huh?"

Denny looked at me. "Who the fuck asked you?"

"It's just that Saturday's kind of unpredictable, you know? Customers can show up any time." I glanced at the door. "Sometimes a whole carload at once."

Robin glanced at the door. "Yeah, Denny. We got the cash. Let's split."

"Nobody comes here this time on Saturday. I told you. I watched this shit box for the last two weeks."

"So what? We got the cash, ain't we?"

Denny threw away the scrap of cloth and grabbed Bett by her hair. "Take off your fucking pants."

She fumbled with her jeans and got them off while Denny held her by her hair and watched. Then she took off her panties. She clutched them in a wad in her hand, so they couldn't be snatched away.

Denny pulled her back on the stool. "Show Robin your pussy."

She shut her eyes tight against the shame and spread her legs. Tears shone on her cheeks.

Robin glared at his brother. "What did you do that for, Denny?"

"If I don't teach you how to be a man, who's going to?"

"You never said nothing about this."

"Are you just going to stand there?" Denny asked. "Ain't you going to fuck her?"

"You said some guys were after you."

"Do I have to show you how?"

"You said I had to help you get some cash to pay them off."

"Your girl went to the prom with a nigger. You never even had the guts to ask her."

"What's the use asking? Nobody wants nothing to do with me. Everybody knows you're my brother."

"A nigger's taking your girl home."

"No girl would go home with me…"

"He's got her down in Coon Hollow by now."

"…because Denny might be there…"

"Him and his friends."

"…and Denny might get weird."

"They're having a three way on her."

Robin's gun made a small pop. It wasn't much of a sound. It seemed like it should have been louder. Denny let go of Bett's hair and sat down hard on the floor. He coughed once, way down in his lungs. Blood came up.

The shot startled Bett's eyes open. She stood down from the stool and tried to back away. She backed into the counter.

Robin looked at her. He looked at me. "He shouldn't have started in on me."

"He should have done it," I agreed. "It wasn't right."

Robin went and stood over his brother. "I told you not to start in on me."

Denny tried to say something. He made a noise in his throat. Blood ran from both corners of his mouth.

"It wasn't right." Robin put his gun against his brother's head and pulled the trigger.

Denny jerked once. He fell over and lay still.

Bett tried to scream. A tiny shriek was all that came out. Piss ran down her leg.

I wanted to run, but my legs felt weak. I hung on to the counter so I wouldn't fall down. I didn't know if Robin was going to shoot me, but I didn't want to fall down.

He just looked at me, kind of sad and scared at the same time. "Will they ever let me out of prison?"

"I don't know," I said. "Maybe. I just don't know about those things."

His shoulders sagged. "I guess it don't matter. I never would have had no life anyway. Not with Denny around."

He shuffled out of the *Nite Spot* like they already had leg irons on him. The night and the rain swallowed him as if he had never existed.

END

Amateur Night

"Flunking isn't a relevant concept anymore," Morrie told his mother. "The University is on strike."

"You haven't gone to your classes," she said in a voice as tense as the lines in her face. "You didn't take your finals."

"Haven't you heard about the Vietnam War?" Morrie asked. "Didn't you hear about the students killed at Kent State?"

"We were all heartbroken by that."

"It's not enough to be liberal," Morrie said. "You have to be radical."

Tears of frustration dampened her eyes. "But you did so well in your first year. Your grades were so good. I was so proud of you."

"I'm not a freshman anymore."

It was no use talking about it. She was living on hopes and expectations from the Depression. From World War II. She was part of the establishment. She would never understand how his generation was changing the world. Morrie was part of the struggle to liberate the oppressed. Part of the New Mobilization. He had to get back to the picket lines. He snatched his coat off the hook and left the house.

He got off the bus half a block from the main gate of the University. Something was wrong. There were no protesters. A maintenance crew was loading the barrels the strikers had used for a makeshift barricade onto a flatbed truck.

"No!" Morrie yelled at them.

They ignored him. Like they didn't even know he was there. He was helpless alone. The nearest source of reinforcements was the East Gate. He took off through the campus at a dead run.

He made it in record time. There were hardly any students. The East Gate was open and empty. Morrie went to each of the other gates. They were deserted. He saw only a few students. There was no use asking them. They were going to the last finals of the semester. They didn't get it. They had no sense that they were scabbing on their fellow workers.

A lot of radical students hung out off campus at a place they called *The Petri Dish*. The food sucked, but you could buy a baggie of grass there. You could roll a joint and light up and nobody said anything. It was close to noon when Morrie got there, but the place was practically empty. The only person he sort of recognized was a girl he had seen at a couple of protests.

He didn't know her name, only that she was hot and she only hung out with the protest leaders. She sat alone at a table. Draped over a chair. Getting high. Letting smoke from her joint out in a long, languid cloud. Morrie worked up his nerve and took his baggie of grass over to the table.

"Mind if I sit here?" he asked.

She considered him with lazy blue eyes. Interested, sort of. Like someone who had spotted a strange new bug on a window sill. She didn't say anything. Just shrugged. More with her eyebrows than her shoulders.

Morrie sat down. He put his baggie on the table and dug out a cigarette paper.

"I was just at the U," he said. "I didn't see any strikers."

"Semester's over," she said.

Her voice was soft and husky, and it had an effect in Morrie's jeans. He concentrated on rolling his joint so he wouldn't be obvious noticing she wasn't wearing a bra under her tie-dyed pullover.

"The strike was supposed to keep the school shut down over break," he said. "That's what everyone was talking about at the last tactics meeting."

"Tactics?" she asked.

She made it sound like a joke. Made him feel like a joke.

"I put my faith in the people," Morrie said. "The people let me down."

It took him two angry tries to fire his lighter and get the joint going. The girl watched him. A little more interested now. She brushed a tendril of blonde hair back from her face.

"It's not enough to be radical," she said. "You have to be revolutionary."

"Yeah?"

That didn't some out right. Morrie wanted to sound cool, but the marijuana high hadn't kicked in yet. His anger showed through.

"They'll be talking about it at *Jo-Jo's* tonight," the girl said, mocking him with her eyes as well as her voice. "If you think you can handle it."

She stubbed out the remains of her joint in an ashtray. Morrie watched her stand up and leave. Even high she was poetry in tight jeans.

He wanted to make it with her. He wanted to show her he was as good as the dudes she hung out with.

Morrie's high didn't linger, and it left him with a buzzing head. Another batch of sorry grass. Another rip off. One more bummer in a bad day. He headed back to the campus.

Some radicals lived in the dorms. They might know why the strike wasn't happening. The first two he tried had already moved out. The third was packing.

"Sure, I can relate to the Movement," he told Morrie. "Only what's the point of a picket line if nobody's trying to cross it?"

"What about the tactics meeting? We talked about it. Everybody agreed. The strike had to go on."

"Yeah, well if some people want to do that I guess it's cool for them. I mean, I can relate."

Morrie felt he air go out of him. It wasn't about relating. You had to believe, and it seemed like he was the only one who did.

He spent the rest of the afternoon wandering. The rallies were over. The campus was nearly empty. The cafeteria in the Student Union Building was closed until next semester, so he had to settle for a sandwich from the food machine for dinner.

Morrie had heard of *Jo-Jo's*. It wasn't a place where student radicals hung out. It was way off campus, like down town. Morrie sort of knew where it was. At least he knew which bus to get on.

It was getting dark when he got down town. The neighborhood was unfamiliar. Probably sketchy even in daylight. Morrie had to remind himself the people who prowled the sidewalks were the way they were because they were oppressed by the system. They were the ones he was struggling to liberate. Dim-lit concrete stairs took him down from the sidewalk and under a bit of hissing neon into *Jo-Jo's*.

It took his eyes a minute to adjust to the dim interior. It wasn't the hippie hangout he had visualized. No bongo drums. No one reading relevant poetry. No chicks in leotards hustling espresso. Just a cavern with posters decorating the brick walls. Hard core stuff. Che Gueverra and like that.

The furniture was bare tables and spindly chairs. Some of the tables had been drawn together in the back. Most of the chairs were occupied by men. They were a few years older than Morrie. They looked older than that. Morrie had grown his hair long, but it came out blond and stringy. His skin was pale and his mustache barely qualified for the name. At campus rallies it didn't matter that he looked like a kid. A lot of radicals did. Here he felt puny and conspicuous.

A few women were scattered among the group, dressed as they pleased, long haired and free of make-up. The girl from *The Petri Dish* was one of them. Morrie drifted uncertainly in her direction. She didn't notice him. She was focused on a guy who was standing up and talking.

His name was Rick. Morrie had seen him at a couple of campus rallies. He was always the dude with the bull horn. The rap was his father was a judge in some rich county.

"Now is the time to make our move," Rick said. "Right now. Tonight. Everybody hates Nixon. They hate the war. The country is a powder keg. All we need to do is light the fuse to start the Revolution."

There was talk. Opinions. Disagreements about which targets to hit. What they should blow up to set off the Revolution. These dudes were Weather Underground.

"Still think you can handle it?"

The girl was standing beside him, challenging him with her eyes. He didn't like being mocked, but the question had already started gnawing at him. He had committed himself to the student strike. His fellow workers had failed him. It would take more than rallies and chanting to drive meaningful change.

"Yeah," he decided. "I can handle it."

"Let's find out."

He felt a foot taller when she took his arm. Rick had a Microbus. The girl sat in front with him. Morrie sat on the floor in back with an assortment of back packs and cartons. He was sitting too low to see anything except passing lights through the windows above.

Their destination was a quiet street uptown flanked by genteel older apartment buildings. It took the three of them two trips to carry the cartons and back packs up to a third floor flat where revolutionary posters decorated the walls. They tore open cartons of dynamite, blasting caps, batteries, wire and kitchen timers.

"Okay," Rick said to Morrie. "Each back pack is we make up into one bomb. Cherry and I will watch to make sure no one hassles you while you plant them. So, you're ready for this, right?"

"Yeah," Morrie said. If there was going to be change, someone had to make it happen.

The damage was done when Police Commissioner Stein arrived on scene. Part of the brick façade of a townhouse was blown out, exposing the interior of an upper floor apartment. The remains of walls and shredded furniture were visible only as grotesque shapes and shadows in the lights from the street.

Police cruisers and yellow tape had an entire block cordoned off. Fire vehicles occupied the middle of the street. The fire was out, but an acrid residue of smoke still hung in the air. Stein had to find his way through a minefield of rubble scattered on the sidewalk to locate the Fire Battalion Commander.

"I was notified there was a bomb squad call-out at this incident," he said.

"Engine Two Nine went in to check for casualties and douse any hot spots," the Battalion Commander said. "They said the apartment looked like some kind of bomb factory. Revolutionary posters on the walls, what was left of them. Weather Underground garbage. Explosives and wires all over the place. They got out fast and we called it in."

"Casualties?" Stein asked.

"Limited to three inside the apartment. Two male, one female, according to the neighbors."

"Were you able to get them out?"

"Engine Two Nine said not worth the risk to try. Bodies were visible. Unrecognizable. Catastrophic trauma. All three."

Stein let out a resigned sigh. "The bomb squad trains for years and they still use a robot to handle explosives. Damn fool kids stuff their heads full of crackpot politics and think they can blow up the world."

"Not this time," the Battalion Commander said. "Amateur night was last week."

END

Conspiracy Theory

i

The fortunate few privileged to wear the coveted green jacket of the *McKnight Messenger Service* will find themselves welcome everywhere in our nation's capitol.

Paul had known that was crap when he hired on. The coveted green jacket was a cheap windbreaker with the company name on the back and the outline of a knight on the front. The company was owned by a greedy little bowling ball of a man. A foreign guy who had changed his name to Martin McKnight.

Okay, so it was all phony. So what? Jobs were scarce, and this one was in D.C. Where the action was. Where the power was. Where he had a chance to finally get the big break he deserved.

Paul was on the sixth floor of the brand new Watergate Tower. In the reception area of the Democratic National Committee. Waiting for the Chairman to come out and sign for a delivery.

The Chairman wasn't alone when he came out. The man with him was short and beefy. His suit didn't fit him very well. No suit ever would.

Paul decided the man was a union official. Paul didn't like unions. He had been forced to join one to keep his supermarket box boy job in high school.

He had enlisted in the Air Force right out of high school to beat the

Vietnam War draft. No more box boy. He was going to be somebody. Maybe learn air traffic control. Maybe even get into officer school. He never should have checked typing on the skill sheet. It cost him four years of his life as a maintenance inventory specialist at an air base in the middle of nowhere.

The Union Official had his own complaint.

"I picked a broad out of your picture book," he said, pointing at a lower drawer in the receptionist's desk. "I get to the Continental Plaza and I find out she ain't working. She's sick, they say. Her replacement tells me fifty for a hand job. A hundred she'll blow me. I mean, Christ, the broad wasn't even white."

The Chairman just smiled. "I'm sorry if there was an issue with the service provider, but all we can do is offer referrals to our out of town colleagues."

"Yeah," the Union Official snarled. "Well, next time somebody better come across. That's all I gotta say. Somebody better come across."

He slammed the door on his way out.

The Chairman scribbled a signature on Paul's delivery ticket and took his package. Not a word to Paul. Hardly even a glance to acknowledge he was there. Another reminder he was nobody. Just a coveted green jacket.

ii

Deliveries to the newspapers were always a pain. The receptionists couldn't sign for anything. All they could do was tell Paul generally where to find the addressee in the maze of offices and cubicles. He had to depend on his messenger jacket and the charity of anyone willing to jerk a thumb in the right direction.

This packet must have been a big deal. It was addressed to an associate editor and the guy had an office with a small window next to the door. Paul saw him inside, sitting alone at his desk and talking on the phone.

Paul opened the door cautiously and let himself in. He hoped his messenger jacket would spare him a bawling out. He was in luck. The Associate Editor was saving his venom for whoever was on the other end of the phone call.

"What the hell kind of headline is that?" he demanded. "It should have said something like 'Break in at Democratic Headquarters'. Make the reader curious. Don't give away the whole story on the top line. Don't you people know how to sell newspapers?"

Paul had seen the story in the morning paper. Five men had been arrested breaking into the Democratic National Committee headquarters in the Watergate Tower. The same place he had been just a couple of weeks ago.

The Associate Editor motioned Paul toward his desk.

"I don't care if the reporter used to be an officer in the Navy. I don't care if he worked in the White House. He was too damn green to be holding down the night desk. How did he get the story, anyway?"

Paul took out the delivery package and put it on the desk.

"No police source just calls the night desk," the Associate Editor was saying. "They don't give away stories for nothing. They want a favor in return. What is it?"

He scribbled a signature in Paul's receipt book, and waved him out.

"Crapola," he said into the phone. "This was some kind of fucking set-up."

Paul put the receipt book away in his pouch and left. Nobody cared what he heard, or overheard. He was just a coveted green jacket.

iii

Messengers weren't allowed breaks, but everyone took them when they got a chance. There was a Howard Johnson's across from the Watergate Tower. Paul went into the coffee shop. They were just bussing tables after the breakfast rush, so he had his choice. He took one where he could see Watergate.

"Is that where it happened?" he asked when the waitress came. "I mean the story in the morning paper."

"Yeah. It was weird. Cops dressed up like hippies busting guys in suits and ties."

"How would you know?" the busboy asked. "You weren't even here."

"I talked to Roxy," she said. "She was on shift then."

"Roxy don't know shit. She just likes to talk."

"She knew about the cops dressed up like hippies. She heard that from Ewald."

"The pusher?"

"Yeah. He came in to get off the street. He said the cops weren't acting like usual. They were kind of hanging around, like they expected something to happen. Ewald took a table near the can, in case he had to flush his load."

"Okay," the busboy said in a snide voice. "If Ewald said so."

"And there was another guy in here, watching the Tower. Ewald knew who he was. Said he got busted off the FBI for juicing. Roxy seen him a couple times with that woman, Kathie what's her name, that runs the hookers over at the Continental Plaza."

"Horse shit," the busboy said, and pushed his cart away.

Paul opened the newspaper he had cribbed from the bus cart and read the story about the break-in again. The burglars were busted in the same room where he had made the delivery.

iv

It seemed like everywhere Paul went there was some jerk who wanted to give him a hard time. High school. The supermarket. The Air Force. At the messenger service it was Randy. The guy was six feet three inches tall, with a moronic laugh and an IQ to match.

"See-Eye-Yay," Randy announced when he came into the lunch room where Paul and two other messengers were eating.

"That's where I delivered," he said while he dug a brown bag out of the refrigerator. "Out where the spies are."

He plunked himself into the plastic chair across the table from Paul.

"Pick-up at the Continental Plaza, where the high class hooers work out of. You know what a hooer is, Paulie?"

Paul ignored the question. With Randy, all you could do was ignore him. It didn't help much.

"Little Paulie's pretending he don't know what hooers are," Randy confided to the other two messengers.

Paul went on eating. He wasn't going to be baited, no matter how nasty Randy got.

"Videotapes," Randy told the other two messengers. "That's what it felt like in the envelope. Square and real light weight. Videotapes of big shots fucking hooers. That's what it was. Isn't that right, Paulie?"

"How would I know?" Paul asked. It wasn't much, but it was a chance to get in a shot.

"Little Paulie don't know about fucking hooers," Randy told the others. "Little Paulie is too scared to fuck hooers. Isn't that right, Paulie?"

Paul finished his sandwich, glad of an opportunity to get away from Randy.

"Be a good little boy, Paulie. Don't fuck no hooers."

Moronic laughter followed him out.

v

It was the end of March. Winter had come and gone and with it Paul's hope of ever getting a big break. Sure, he could go anywhere in the city, but when he got there he was just a nothing messenger.

Today was no different. Another office. Another empty reception area. Another package that required a signature.

He heard voices on the other side of a connecting door. Two men. He thought about knocking, but one of the voices was angry, accusing.

"They're fucking spies, all of them. Don't spies know to keep their mouths shut?"

"You don't know that."

"It's all over the papers. The guys doing the break-in were Cubans. Bay of Pigs. CIA. All that shit."

The two men were arguing about the Watergate trial. It had been in the morning papers. One of the burglars had written some kind of confession to the judge.

"So one of them decided not to take the rap."

"That whole arrest smells sour. When the cops get a burglary call they send the uniform who drives that beat. They don't call the vice squad. And one of those cops used to be hooked up with the CIA."

"The guy said in the letter to the judge the CIA wasn't involved."

"Bullshit. Who bothers to mention the CIA in a letter to a judge? If they didn't put him up to it, why did he even bother mentioning them?"

"What does the CIA get out of it?"

"They hate this administration. They set the burglars up to get busted to make trouble. The cops and the judge were too stupid to get the picture. They had their own guy rat it out."

Paul felt a chill run up his spine. These two guys were mixed up in Watergate. They must be, from the way they were talking.

"May I help you?"

It was a woman's voice, crisp enough to make Paul jump. A hatchet-faced receptionist had returned and caught him eavesdropping.

"Messenger service," he blurted. "I need a signature."

Paul completed the delivery and got out of there, but he couldn't get the conversation out of his head. He remembered the Associate Editor saying the arrests were some kind of set-up.

vi

The building was one of those Federal labyrinths. Paul paused to check the number on the door to be sure he had the right office. Male voices came from inside.

"I don't think this guy is giving us a straight story. There are parts of it that just don't tally."

"It doesn't matter. We need a stellar witness. This guy is perfect for the role."

"He's in front of the Watergate investigating committee on national television. If someone asks him the wrong question, it could blow everything."

"We'll be asking the questions."

Paul felt a hand close around his arm and jerked around to see a thick-set man in a security uniform.

"Here, what do you think you're doing in this building?"

The door opened and two men in suits looked out.

"What's going on here?" one suit asked.

"Messenger service," Paul managed to blurt out. He read the name on the delivery slip. "I need a signature."

"Oh, it's okay," the suit told the security guard. "I've been expecting this."

The guard released Paul.

"Bring it in," the suit told Paul.

The office wasn't small, but it was stacked and strewn with file folders until there was barely room to move. The suit found a pen on a desk and scribbled a signature on the receipt, talking to the other man while he did.

"They crapped on us in the election," he said. "Now it's our turn to crap on them. Crap for crap. That's how it is in this town."

Paul was shaking when he left the building. He had been watching the Watergate hearings on television. Reading the newspapers. The suit was right. It was all crap.

Everything Paul had heard and overheard came rushing back to him. It all began to take shape, and he began to realize what Watergate was really all about. Maybe he was the only one in D.C. who did.

His big break had finally come. The one he had waited and hoped for.

vii

"Just put it on the desk," the Editor said when Paul stepped into his office.

Like Paul wasn't a real person. Like he was just a green messenger jacket. That was about to change.

"This isn't a delivery," Paul said.

The Editor glanced up irritably.

Paul knew he had to talk fast. His messenger jacket had allowed him to walk into the newspaper offices unchallenged, but he would be escorted out just as quickly if he didn't prove he had legitimate business there.

"It's about Watergate," he said.

The Editor looked him over skeptically.

"That stuff on TV," Paul said, summoning all the courage he could muster. "That hearing. It's all wrong."

Once he got going, words tumbled out of Paul's mouth as he told the

Editor what he had learned and pieced together over the past weeks. The drawer full of prostitutes' pictures in the very room where the burglars were caught. The strange behavior of the police before they caught the men. The delivery of videotapes of prostitutes and important men to the CIA.

"All the burglars were in the CIA once," Paul said. "One of the cops who arrested them was in the CIA once."

That's what it was really about. Watergate. It wasn't about politics at all. It was about hookers and spies. Paul has overheard people talking about the CIA setting the whole thing up because they hated the administration. He had overheard the suits saying the key witness in the Senate hearing wasn't telling the whole truth. He laid it all out for the Editor, and waited full of anticipation for the man's response.

"The door is behind you," the Editor said, and went back to his work.

Paul fumbled for words, but none came out. Leaden feet took him out of the office before security could come to remove him

viii

Paul didn't understand the Editor's reaction. He had explained everything. He hadn't held anything back. Maybe he had spoken too fast. Maybe things had come out garbled.

That was it. That must be it. He had a habit of talking too fast when he was excited. He should have written it all down. Rehearsed it. Memorized it.

Then he had a better idea.

He would write it all down, but as a newspaper story. He would hand it to the Editor. That way it would appear under his name. All the fame would be his. He would be interviewed on TV for blowing the lid off Watergate. There would be a million dollar book deal.

The outline of the article was already forming in his head when he checked in at the messenger service to pick up his deliveries.

"Mr. McKnight wants to see you," the receptionist told him. "In his office."

The little bowling ball was sitting in his leather chair, dwarfed by the massive, polished desk in front of him.

"Have you anything to say for yourself," he demanded.

Paul stared in confusion.

"I just received a very disturbing telephone call from the Editor of the city's premier newspaper. He said you barged into his office with a preposterous conspiracy theory."

Paul was stunned. Newspapers were supposed to keep their sources confidential. All right. If that was the way the Editor wanted to play it, there were other newspapers in D.C. His messenger jacket would grant him entry to any of them.

"You have besmirched the honored name of the *McKnight Messenger Service*," the Bowling Ball said. "You are no longer privileged to wear the coveted green jacket."

END

The Street

Bird Leg never saw where they came from. One minute he was hurrying along the sidewalk, hands in his pockets and shoulders hunched against the bitter South Chicago wind. The next minute they had him by the arms, shoving him into a doorway.

There were three of them. Disciples. Gang bangers. Everybody on the street knew who they were.

Bird Leg was taller than any of them, but he was skin and bones. Karate was all muscle, bulked up, like he lived in a gym. Tony Go was jittery, he never stopped moving. Monster was broad, hulking, shapeless.

"Where you going?" Monster asked.

"Fo' a walk," Bird Leg lied.

They didn't say anything. They just stared at him. They didn't believe him.

"Just fo' a walk," he repeated.

"You going to meet Shimmy," Tony Go said.

"No," Bird Leg insisted. "Just fo' a walk."

"You going to whack him for us," Karate said.

"What you say?" Bird Leg asked.

"You going to whack Shimmy for us," Tony Go said.

"I don't whack nobody," Bird Leg said. "I don't know how."

"You got a cute little sister," Karate said.

"If you don't do like we say," Monster said, "we take her down in the hole."

"We fuck her," Tony Go said. "Until we can't fuck no more."

Karate put the blade of a knife against Bird Leg's cheek. "Then we fix her face so don't nobody ever want to fuck her again. Not never."

Bird Leg felt his stomach start to seethe. He fought to keep it from erupting.

Tony Go jitterbugged, grinning, and showed Bird Leg a small gun. "You know how to work this? This here's the safety. You push down. Then you pulls the trigger."

"You get up close," Karate said. "Kill him in the head."

Monster made a gun out of his fingers and put it to Bird Leg's temple and pretended to fire. Tony Go put the real gun in the pocket of Bird Leg's jacket.

"Don't forget your sister," Karate said, and then they were gone.

Bird Leg retraced his steps. Fear pushed his pace to a trot. A ghetto blaster was going as he neared The Projects. The kids were leaving for school, the girls switching their hips in time with the music.

"Don't do that," he said.

He was across the street, too far away for them to hear, but he said it anyway. He had warned his sister, Shawna, against it. Against acting sexy. She just laughed at him, like she and her friends knew better than he did. She was thirteen now. She and her friends, they thought it was all just giggles and teasing boys. The pimps cruising in their big, square Lincolns were bound to notice her one of these first days.

Bird Leg watched until she came out of their building. She and a group of girls. Grandma Alice and the old ladies in The Projects, they were too smart to let girls go out alone. Even just to walk to school.

Bird Leg followed for a block or so, across the street where he wouldn't be noticed. Sometimes he wished he was still in school. He was never good in the classes. At least not good so the teachers or anyone else would notice. That didn't matter so much. He had felt safe when he was in school.

When he was fifteen he started hearing the taunts. He could still hear them, echoing in his head.

"School ain't nuffin'."

"Yo gets yo respec' on the street."

"Yo gots to be able to handle the street."

He had quit going to school. The same time as his friend Shimmy. Bird Leg didn't know what to do with himself, but Shimmy always had ideas.

He was going to be late meeting Shimmy.

Bird Leg ran the last two blocks to the old house. It was mostly burned down now. The dopers used it after it was abandoned and it caught fire one night.

Shimmy was waiting just inside the charred remains of the doorway, just like always. He looked sharp, just like always. New sneakers, brand name, with the laces untied. Raiders jacket. Baseball cap with the bill turned to the side over one ear.

"Where you been? Shimmy demanded.

"I'm here, ain't I?"

"The Post Office be opening in a few minutes," Shimmy said. "They mamas be coming out wif they food stamps."

Bird Leg squirmed. "Maybe we shouldn't be doin' this, you know. Food stamps is supposed to be for food."

"They mamas, they don't care about no food. They want they drugs. That's all they want."

Shimmy was smart about those things. He knew where to sell the food stamps, and how much money to get for them. Shimmy thrust the envelope at Bird Leg. The envelope with the buy money in it.

"Don't you be giving them no fifty cents on the dollar."

"I know," Bird Leg said.

"Just enough for they next couple hits. That's all."

"I know." Bird Leg put the envelope away inside his jacket.

"And you make sure you get all they stamps. They mamas, they sneaky. Don't let them hold out on you."

Bird Leg just shrugged.

"We got to hurry," Shimmy said. "If we don't get they food stamps, they gang bangers will."

Shimmy put his head out the doorway and looked both directions, just like he always did. That was when Bird Leg shot him.

He put the gun to the back of his friend's head and pushed the safety down and pulled the trigger. The tiny pistol made a sharp crack, not like the distant popping of gunfire he had heard before on the street. The smoke burned his nostrils.

Shimmy fell down in the doorway, fell on his side so he was looking

61

up at Bird Leg. He was still alive, and he was looking up at Bird Leg with eyes full of disbelief.

Bird Leg shot him again to make him stop. And again and again.

"I'm sorry, man," Bird Leg said. "I meant no disrespect by it."

Shimmy was gone, but his eyes were still open and staring. Bird Leg stepped over him and went out through the charred doorway, but he could still feel the eyes on him. He turned and went back.

"I meant no disrespect by it," he yelled down at Shimmy.

There was no answer. He put the little gun away in his pocket and left.

There were people out walking, but no one said anything. This was the street. No one ever said anything. No one saw anything. No one did anything.

Bird Leg didn't go to the Post Office. He just walked. Aimlessly. For a long time.

It was evening when he got back to The Projects. To Grandma Alice's. The old woman and his sister were there, making dinner.

"Where you been, Bird Leg?" his sister asked.

"Don't you be calling him that," Grandma Alice scolded. "His name is Shawn. Just like yours is Shawna. Your mother gave you those names, before the angels came and took her up to heaven."

It wasn't angels that took their mother. It was paramedics. Bird Leg could still remember their talk.

"This is the third OD tonight," one said.

"Must be some bad shit on the street," the other said.

Neither of them seemed to care. To them it was just another night in The Projects. They covered Bird Leg's mother all over with a sheet and took her down in the freight elevator because the gurney wouldn't fit in the regular ones. After that it had been up to Grandma Alice to look after Bird Leg and his sister.

Bird Leg took a ten dollar bill out of his pocket. It was from the buy money. He put it on the kitchen counter.

Grandma Alice didn't touch it. "I don't want none of that filth in my house."

"I got it doing a errand," Bird Leg said.

"You get it out of here and wash yourself up for dinner," the old woman said.

Bird Leg snatched the money. "No. If you don't want no ten dollars I got doing a errand, I don't want no dinner."

He went out and down the hall and into the stairwell. The stairwell smelled from everybody who had pissed or taken a shit there, but it was too early for the dopers to come, so he could be alone.

There was no one to see his tears. No one to hear him when he said, "I'm sorry, man. I meant no disrespect by it."

END

Wall Street

A sudden movement startled the old man. The black cat had landed noiselessly on the corner of his desk. He grinned at his frayed nerves. "Hello, Jinx," he said. "How's my favorite kitty?"

The animal ignored the greeting, curled into a routing box and began washing a hind leg with long, languid strokes of its tongue, oblivious to the storm that lashed the night outdoors and rattled the window in its casement.

The old man resumed his scrutiny, removing his spectacles to peer at the entries on the settlement sheet. He had to be sure before he drove into the city tomorrow to confront the brokerage firm.

Jinx the cat stopped its tongue in mid-stroke. An instant later the animal was up on all four paws. Its back arched. Fur bristled along its spine. It leaped off the desk and scurried from the room.

The old man went cold with terror. Had they really come to silence him? He retrieved an automatic pistol and a box of bullets from a desk drawer.

The pistol was a relic of his youth. Taken from a fallen German. Kept as an illicit war trophy. Dredged up from a trunk full of memories when the threats began. The bullets were new. He dropped more than one fumbling them into the magazine. Passing years had robbed his hands of strength. It took three tries to rack the slide far enough to chamber a round. He de-cocked the weapon and listened.

The big old house had been his home for decades. He knew every sound it made, down to the tiniest squeak. He heard nothing out of the ordinary. The intruders had not yet violated his sanctuary. He found a coat and a hat and went out into the storm to intercept them.

The grounds covered an acre. The house was set well back from the little-travelled road in front. At the rear was shoreline and beyond that lay the open water of Long Island Sound. Mature hedges rustled in the wind and screened the neighbors on either side. The only light leaked from his own curtained windows. He had forgotten his spectacles, but they would be useless in the wind-driven rain. He made his way around the house.

A night light burned above the rear porch. Two of Wall Street's finest were absorbed in a clumsy effort to pry open the kitchen door.

The brokerage firm had touted them highly. Logan was the younger, a former college athlete and a fierce competitor. Maples was a seasoned professional. Just the team to shepherd the old man's fortune.

It wasn't long before unauthorized transactions began appearing in his settlement sheets. Blue chip stocks were sold and high risk bonds bought in their place. When he complained, he was told he was being foolish. He was ungrateful. Logan and Maples were going to make him more money than he had ever made. When he insisted the transactions be reversed, the threats began.

"May I help you, gentlemen?" he asked.

Both men froze. Their heads swiveled in unison. They peered into the dimness below the porch, furtively at first and then curiously.

"It's him," Maples realized.

"Yeah," Logan said grimly.

Both voices had the jittery edge of cocaine.

The two men came carefully down from the porch, as if exposure to the bare overhead bulb had compromised their night vision. The old man stood his ground, holding the pistol out of view in his coat pocket.

"You look different without the pinstripes and the power ties," he remarked. "I guess the life jackets mean you came by boat?"

The trip must have been planned in advance. The shoreline scouted in daylight so they could find their way at night. The old man listened for the thunk of a hull washing against the estate's finger pier. His ears caught only the noise of the storm.

The two men found a semblance of footing on the soft, slippery grass. Surprise had passed. Assurance began to assert itself.

"We told you not to make trouble," Logan said.

What did they expect? The money was his legacy. It was all he had to preserve his dignity in the years ahead. To help his family over any rough patches. To ensure college for his grandchildren.

"Do you think silencing me will save you?" the old man asked. "There must be other accounts like mine. Gradually drained of sound investments. High risk bonds taking their place. How many? Dozens? Hundreds?"

"This is the nineteen eighties," Logan said. "The old rules don't apply."

"Growth is what matters now," Maples said. "High yield requires high risk. Investors have to accept that risk and remain confident."

To these two the old man was just one more source of fuel for their ambitions. His complaints only a speed bump on their career paths.

"No," was all he said.

"It's all about confidence," Logan said. "If one client rocks the boat, it rattles every client."

"It takes investor confidence to maintain the momentum," Maples said.

"It takes guts," Logan said.

Forty two years it had been, the old man calculated, since he had gone ashore at Normandy. He had been a year out of Princeton. A Second Lieutenant's bar on one collar and the crossed rifles of the infantry on the other. One of many souls crammed into the stark, steel interior of a landing craft. Waves tossed them mercilessly. Blowing spray drenched everyone. A soup of salt water and vomit sloshed around their boots. Then came the bullets and the bleeding. Terror was coin of the realm. It was a day when courage couldn't be measured by the audacity of your deceit.

"Have you ever killed anyone?" the old man asked.

It wasn't a question he had meant to ask. He had simply blurted out the worst of his fears.

The two men fidgeted, and made it real.

"It's not like we want to do this," Maples said.

"We're risking everything," Logan said. "Our careers. Families. Everything."

"We could go to prison," Maples said

"Better if there's an accident," Logan said. "You just bump your head and wash up on some beach."

"You brought it on yourself," Maples said.

Logan was already advancing, hefting the pry bar and raising it over his head. Only when the old man felt the automatic pistol buck in his hand was he aware that he had taken it out of his pocket.

The impact of the bullet reduced Logan to a rag doll. He sagged to his knees and pitched forward. Maples' attempt to retreat came too late. The old man had already fired again. A second reflexive shot on the heels of the first.

Maples stumbled back against the railing of the porch steps. He tried to regain his footing, but his strength failed. His bulk oozed down and came to rest in a sitting position, lopsided and flaccid.

Only the old man remained standing. The jolt of adrenaline that had spurred him to action drained away. He began to shiver from emotional shock.

Jinx the cat appeared in the dim light, a sleek black figure sodden from the storm. The animal had ventured out to meet the threat to its territory. It crept close to each of the men, exploring them in turn.

"Don't worry, kitty," the old man said. "They'll be gone soon enough."

He had seen sucking chest wounds on the battlefield. The thoracic cavity was punctured and air rushed in through the penetration. Unless the wounds were plugged immediately with a non-porous material the lungs would collapse and death would follow quickly. Too quickly for him to do anything about it. Even if he wanted to.

Logan and Maples had come to take his life. Not out of any hatred or personal conviction. Simply for profit. They had probably thought it would be easy. A wretched night. An isolated estate. An old man living alone with his cat.

The episode had left him dazed. His ears were ringing from the report of the automatic. The web of his hand stung from the recoil. He put the weapon away in his pocket and stood waiting for lights to come on in the neighboring houses. For the sirens of emergency vehicles.

He had no idea what he would say to the police. Or how he would explain this to his family. For decades he had lived quietly, without drama or incident. He had no experience dealing with either.

Minutes passed with nothing but wind and rain. His hearing began to recover. Somewhere in the distance a branch let go with a crack not unlike the noise of a gunshot. It began to seem possible that the storm had swallowed the reports of the pistol.

The old man began to think, slowly at first, carefully and logically. Logan and Maples were criminals certainly, but fools only to a point. They were right when they said Wall Street depended on confidence. A scandal would bring detractors out of the woodwork, preening and strutting, gloating over how right they had been, while good people who had entrusted their savings would suffer the consequences. Wall Street had to be protected, even from its own criminal stupidity.

The threat of exposure might well be enough to frighten them into quietly putting the accounts right. But the necessary level of discretion could be maintained only if the activities of Logan and Maples never came under public scrutiny.

It took some hunting in the basement to find the Radio Flyer wagon the old man had used to pull his granddaughter around the grounds when she was little. There was some rust, and the axles squeaked, but it was serviceable. By a combination of tipping the wagon and tugging the corpse, he was able to get Logan's torso over the center of gravity with all four wheels on the ground.

He thought through the next steps on the laborious trip to the pier, pulling the wagon against the resistance of Logan's trailing arms and legs. It would be dangerous, taking an unfamiliar boat out into the storm, but he had sailed these waters often as a young man. He knew where the currents divided, where flotsam would be carried away and simply disappear into the trackless expanse of the ocean.

Even at night a compass would get him back within sight of the shore. His knowledge of the shoreline would bring him back to the pier. The boat could then be set at half throttle and released out into open water.

The craft would eventually be found. Empty. Bobbing. Out of fuel. A presumed boating mishap would likely be put down to the tragic outcome of a cocaine fueled lark. It would cast no shadow on the victims' professional lives. And it would spare the families of the two dead men the humiliation of a scandal.

It was a crime, of course, but one done without malice and in the service of a greater good.

END

Hard Time

The man was haggy and ill-shaven. A plastic chair had deformed under his bulk. He wore the jump suit of a jail inmate. The chain around his neck was a tattoo. The shackles that fastened his thick wrists to the table were chrome steel.

The woman seated herself across from him. She was petite and prim, her hair a short salon wave. There was a chill in the interview room and she didn't unbutton her topcoat. She put an ebony smart phone on the table and set it to record.

"You are Elmer Perkins?" she asked.

"Bryce," he snapped.

"Excuse me?"

"Bryce. It's my middle name. I go by Bryce. I ain't no fucking Elmer."

"My name is Angela Kay, Mr. Perkins. The court has appointed me to provide you with legal representation."

"So get me the fuck out of here."

"Did the police inform you that you may be charged with murder in the first degree?" she asked.

"I didn't fucking do nothing."

His restraints rattled holding back a burst of anger. She waited until he subsided in frustration and then set a shoulder bag on the table. From that she extracted an official looking document. It was several pages thick.

"You made a statement to the police."

"Yeah. I told them how it was. All of it."

"Were you advised of your right to have an attorney present during your interview?"

"I told you already. I didn't fucking do nothing. Why would I need a lawyer?"

"According to your statement," she said, glance reading while she spoke, "you were involved in a poker game."

"Texas hold-em. Licensed card room. All legal."

"Where you became indebted to a stranger who gave his name as Landrieu?"

"Fat little fucker," Perkins recalled. "Fat fingers with hardly any knuckles on them. All the time sweating. He smelled like he was sweating cologne."

"And you signed over title to a motorcycle to secure the debt?"

"A Harley, lady. A fucking Harley."

"He offered you the opportunity to redeem the title?"

"Do him a favor. That's what he said. Little favor. No big sweat." Resentment had replaced bluster in Elmer Perkins' voice.

"What exactly did he want you to do?" she asked.

"There's this broad. Rich, you know. Fur coat. Big wedding rock. Fancy car. Like that. She's got to go to a place. I'm supposed to go along. Just to make sure everything stays cool, you know. Maybe use a little muscle if anyone hassles her. Nothing heavy, you know."

Faraway voices echoed from the ventilation duct. An unrelated conversation, distorted and barely audible. Angela Kay penciled a few notes on the printed statement.

"And you don't know the woman's name?"

"I asked. She was a looker so I asked. She just keeps driving."

"Where did you go?"

"We stop at this house. Quiet street. All the places are dark. Like everyone's gone to bed."

"Did the woman say anything?"

"Zoltan's going to bless the money. That's all she says. She pops the console. There's a piece inside."

"By a piece, do you mean a pistol?"

"A nine. A Glock. Small one, you know, like you could shove in your pocket. The broad tells me stash it inside my jacket. Then we go up to the house."

"Did she have a key?"

"She hadda ring the bell. This dude in one of those turban things lets us in. Big dude. Like he plays left tackle for the Bombay Bombers or something."

"His name was Zoltan?" Angela Kay asked. Her tone was skeptical.

"That's what the broad called him. Not like they were friends, or like that. Just like, you know, she knew him."

"And he was expecting you?"

"He tells us go in this room. There's this big silver plate on a table. The broad starts pulling cash out of her purse. Bundled up, you know, like from a bank. She puts it on the plate. Kind of arranging it, you know. Then she takes off the fur coat. I mean, like, she's naked underneath. She tells me to get naked too."

"Did you disrobe voluntarily?"

"Yeah. Sure. When it's party time, it's party time."

"What did you do with the pistol?"

"I hadda leave it under my jacket. The broad tells me to carry the plate of cash. We go in this other room. That's when things got weird."

Angela Kay set the statement aside. "Tell me everything you can remember. Take your time. Be as detailed as you can."

"There's this smoke. Like, what do they call it? Incense? And there's this music. Weird sounding, like in the space alien movies, you know. And this Zoltan dude is standing behind this kind of altar thing. That's what he called it. He told me to put the plate with the cash on the altar.

The broad and me stand in front of the altar. The lights get dim. Zoltan, he gets this look. Like he's spaced out, you know. He starts waving his hands over the cash and talking some kind of foreign crap. That's when these two kids come in."

"How old were the children?"

"Old enough, you know. I mean one of them is this cute guy and he starts in on the broad. You know, kissing her nipples and fingering her and like that. The other one is this chick. She starts in on me. You know, like she really digs me."

"Do you mean she performed oral sex on you?"

"Really doing a number on me. I mean, like, the whole room is spinning. When it stops there's just me and this Zoltan dude. He's lying on the floor dead and the piece is on the altar. Still smoking, you know, and--".

"Did you see who shot Zoltan?"

"I never even heard a shot. Everybody else is gone. I figure I better split too. I'm pulling my pants on when this cop crashes in. He keeps yelling 'show me your hands' over and over."

Angela Kay absorbed the information without moving or speaking. The stillness made Perkins visibly nervous.

"I don't get it," he said. "The crap about blessing the cash."

Angela Kay spoke absently, delicately, as if she were drawing her thoughts together like flowers in a bouquet.

"Superstitious gamblers are easy prey for confidence swindlers. Blessing money to bring luck before it is wagered is a common ploy. The ceremony is to make the victim feel important and involved, and to cover a switch of real money for counterfeit."

"You mean all the smoke?"

"Probably blended with a mild narcotic. The altar would contain some means of directing it toward the victim and away from the perpetrator."

"So who whacked that Zoltan dude?"

"I suspect your Mr. Landrieu had won some of the counterfeit and traced the problem back to Zoltan."

"So why didn't he just hire some dudes to beat the crap out of Zoltan and get his bread back?"

"This sort of fraud is usually perpetrated by gangs. Criminal migrants. Gypsies. Irish Travelers. Zoltan was just the public face of the problem. Landrieu needed to eliminate Zoltan in a way that would send a message to those behind him to take their scheme elsewhere. The woman and the money were used to lure Zoltan into staging one of his ceremonies."

"Why send me?"

"To take the blame, Mr. Perkins."

"It ain't like I didn't tell those cops how it was. Twenty times at least. Why don't they bust Landrieu?"

"All the police can do is interview him. He will appear with counsel. He will have a verifiable alibi. He will plead ignorance of criminal matters."

"The rich broad can say how it was."

72

"Landrieu wouldn't have chosen the woman unless he was sure of her silence. She likely has a husband who wouldn't take kindly to her gambling addiction."

"The kids musta seen how it went down."

"Do you know the term 'hammer', Mr. Perkins?"

"Like, what do you mean?"

"Confidence swindlers always run the risk that the victim will complain to the police. The standard method of preventing that is to lure the victim into committing a crime. He can't complain without damning himself. In your case, sexual communication with a minor child."

"I didn't do nothing. It was that little chick doing her number on me."

"You were the adult in a sexual encounter with a minor child. You will be held legally responsible regardless of who initiated or performed the act. If the child is found, you will be convicted. You will be imprisoned for an extended period. You will have to register as a sex offender for the rest of your life."

Perkins' features sagged under the weight of disbelief. He made a half-hearted effort at laughter.

"Hey, come on. I gotta get outta here. I gotta get my Harley back."

"I doubt that it still exists," Angela Kay said.

"What?"

"It is evidence of conspiracy. And most motor vehicles are worth more as parts than as a complete assembly."

"You're telling me they chopped my Harley?"

A rattle of steel reminded Perkins that anger was pointless. He subsided into bitterness.

"You think I'm stupid," he decided. "I don't play by your chicken shit rules so I'm a jerk."

"You've made some poor choices."

Perkins' expression twisted into a sneer. "Fucking college broad, ain't you? Grew up with a silver spoon. You don't know shit about real people."

"How do you suppose I wound up sitting across this table from you, Mr. Perkins?"

"How would I know?"

"I practice corporate law. Sometimes I'm tempted to go the extra mile for a lucrative client. I irritated the wrong judge and wound up serving one hundred hours of community service. I began my career providing legal defense for the indigent. I was sent back out of some warped sense of justice."

"You're doing fucking time here?"

"If you would prefer another attorney, I can obtain a request form from the Public Defender's Office."

Perkins' eyes fidgeted. "This is crazy. Like, everything is back asswards."

"On the contrary, Mr. Perkins. The murder of Zoltan was conceived and executed with exquisite care by someone intimately familiar with both the law and the mechanisms used to enforce it."

Angela Kay danced glossy fingernails on Perkins' statement and made steady eye contact with him.

"Neither of us can change the past. The right choice now will give you a chance at a better future."

"I don't need no lecture. I need some fucking justice."

"As it stands, Mr. Perkins, given your ignorance of the conspiracy, I may be able to persuade the Prosecutor to bargain your case down if you plead guilty to rendering criminal assistance for transporting the pistol."

"Like, down to what?" he asked.

"Sentencing guidelines are fourteen to twenty two months in prison."

"That's hard time," he protested.

His only answer was the echo of distant laughter from the ventilation duct.

END

Public Transit

The fire department medical truck was pulling away when Peter Beaumont arrived. The coppery smell of blood hit him as soon as he got down to the subway platform. The floor was a Rorschach blot of dark stains and a litter of discarded clothing. Beaumont didn't bother to display his badge, just lifted the police tape and ducked under.

The supervising uniform was big Eddie Anastasia. The Sergeant's stripes on his sleeve meant he didn't have to move his four hundred pounds unless he wanted to. He watched Beaumont approach with a bemused smile.

"So, they sent in the heavy artillery," Eddie said.

"Boom," Beaumont said, and opened his folder.

"Which version you want?" Eddie asked.

"Anything that doesn't give me writer's cramp."

"Three victims. Male. Negro. Juvenile. Mid-teens, by my guess."

"Carrying ID?"

"Get real, Beau. This is the nineteen nineties. Switchblades, yeah. Aluminum knucks, yeah. ID, forget it."

Beaumont glanced around the platform. The good news was no fatalities. No bodies lying under tarps waiting for the Medical Examiner.

"Crime scene crew stuck in traffic again?" he asked.

"Either that or it's raining out. Or maybe they had to go to Mass for Saint Swithin's Day. When it comes to alibis, those guys could give the crooks lessons."

"Witnesses?" Beaumont asked.

"Most of the primaries had taken it on the arches by the time we got here. Only suckers get involved. Best I could get from the leftovers, the victims accosted some white dude on the platform."

"Accosted?" Beaumont asked.

"It's a police word," Eddie reminded him. "We're supposed to use it when we're not sure what happened. Which is most of the time."

"Then what?"

"A scuffle ensued. I think that's how we're supposed to say it. White dude hoofs it up the stairs with the rest of the crowd and he's gone."

"Description?"

"Medium average. Jeans. Denim jacket. Cap."

"Anything unusual?"

"Just the cap. He wore it with the bill forward. I mean, who does that anymore?" Beaumont closed the folder. "Okay. I'm going to walk and talk until Crime Scene gets here."

"You know why they sent you, don't you, Beau?"

"Last I heard it was called criminal investigation."

"White guy stabs three black kids," Eddie said. "If the brass don't deliver this dude subito, they're going to take the news media night stick up their asses."

ii

The Chief of Detectives scowled when Beaumont stepped into his office. "Do you know Captain Mason?"

A handsome, heavy-set black in a Captain's uniform was seated beside his desk.

"No, Sir," Beaumont said.

"I read your case notes," the Chief said. "Any update?"

"Medical report. Injuries consistent with a robust, fixed-blade knife."

"Hunting knife? K-Bar?"

"Possibly."

"What are your next steps?"

"Interview the victims. Neighborhood canvass."

"Captain Mason will organize the canvass." The Chief jabbed a finger at the Captain. "Mace, you pull whatever resources you need. Shoe leather up and down the block. Work the phones. Cab companies. Delivery companies. City departments. Anyone who might have had eyes on the street when this went down. We need this perpetrator right now. Christ, we should have had him yesterday."

iii

The victims were still hospitalized. Beaumont decided to start with the youngest.

Dawon Hall's grandmother was thin without being gaunt. She was tall enough to look Beaumont in the eye.

"Dawon is a good boy," she insisted.

"Yes, Ma'am," Beaumont said, and introduced himself to the thin fourteen year old in the hospital bed. "I'd like you to tell me what happened in your own words."

The youth refused to make eye contact. "I feel sorry for they honkies," he declared.

"Can you describe the man who assaulted you? Was there anything distinctive about him?"

No eye contact. "I feel sorry for they daughters."

It was hopeless. Dawon was terrified by the unfamiliar world he found himself in. He had retreated behind the shield of youthful bravado. Beaumont gave a business card to his grandmother.

"His mother was a good mother to him," the elderly woman said. "Only the drugs came and took her away before she could grow him all the way up."

iv

Richie Collins' mother stood protectively between Beaumont and the bed that held her son.

"Why do you want to talk to my boy?" she asked

77

"Your son was the victim of a crime, Ma'am. We're investigating the circumstances."

"I read a newspaper this morning that said those boys were trying to rob that white man."

"I didn't do nothing," came the youthful voice from the bed behind her.

"He gets to have a lawyer before you can talk to him. Isn't that right?"

"Your son is not under investigation for any offense," Beaumont assured her. "We are simply trying to put together the best description we can of the man who assaulted him."

"What good will that do?" the woman asked. "It just means I have to take more time off my work to bus ride him downtown to fill out papers that don't mean anything. Some people from the church are coming bye and bye. We're going to pray on my boy and get him better. That's all that matters."

v

LaTracy Jackson was scheduled for additional surgery. It was another two days before Beaumont could interview him. He was the last realistic opportunity to develop a description of the perpetrator and a victim narrative of events.

His mother was there when Beaumont arrived. She was unremarkable beyond erect posture, and the anger and resentment that filled her eyes when he showed her his credentials.

"What are you doing here, Mister White Policeman? Why aren't you out catching that white man that cut my boy?"

"That's why I'm here, Ma'am. I'd like to ask what he remembers about the man."

"I don't 'member nothin'," the youth said.

His voice was not strong but his tone was the defiance he had learned and practiced on the street. It was all he had to protect him in a hostile urban environment.

The key to breaking through that kind of defense mechanism was to build rapport with the subject. Looming over the boy while he lay in a hospital bed made that impossible.

"Any distinctive detail about how he looked or acted could help us find him."

"Don't 'member."

They were all crowded into a narrow, curtained-off space, LaTracy, his mother and Beaumont. With each question Beaumont asked the boy grew more withdrawn and the woman grew more hostile. He didn't take it personally. She was a mama bear protecting her cub.

"I'm going to get a lawyer and sue all you white policemen," she said as Beaumont left.

vi

The next week produced no results. The Police Commissioner and the Manhattan District Attorney made a televised appeal for the assailant to turn himself in, promising that things would go much harder for him if the police had to track him down. Beaumont and the rest of New York knew it was a pointless act of desperation.

Big Eddie Anastasia was in a foul mood when Beaumont encountered him at the scene of a strong arm sidewalk robbery. It wasn't the chill wind or the persistent drizzle that was bothering him.

"I hear Captain Smoke and the big subway task force goose-egged," he said.

"I haven't heard," Beaumont admitted.

"You're primary on this cluster fuck, ain't you?"

"Do you know how many case files I have open?"

"Spare me the crap, Beau. This guy pulled the old scramola. If he's smart enough to keep his face shut, you ain't gonna catch him."

"Patrol getting a hard time about it?" Beaumont asked.

"It ain't the hard time. It's the overtime. Uniform visibility on the street. Show the citizens they're safe. If you ask me, the brass is having nightmares. They're afraid this guy will give the citizens the idea they can look after themselves."

"You can always retire. Get a few good meals under your belt. Put some meat on those bones."

"Fuck you."

vii

The last of the subway assault victims was wheeled out of the hospital to a fanfare of media criticism of police incompetence. Beaumont was summoned to the Chief of Detectives' office.

"I was in a division house yesterday," the Chief said. "A sign on the white board said 'good guys three, bad guys zero'. What do you think about that?"

"When I was a kid in the service it was 'will the last GI to leave Vietnam please turn out the light at the end of the tunnel'. Now it's 'will the last person to leave New York please turn out the lights on Broadway'. People need a harmless way to let off steam. To deal with things they can't control."

"There is an assailant out there in the city laughing at us right now. Do you call that harmless?"

"The perp is long gone," Beaumont said. "He wasn't a New Yorker."

"You know something you haven't put in the case file?"

"His cap was cited in the notes."

"His cap?"

"He wore it with the bill forward. No New Yorker would do that."

Beaumont didn't know whether the Chief accepted his line of thinking, but the old man had too many years' experience not to know the window for apprehension had closed.

"It is what it is," was all that the Chief conceded. "We can't afford to throw any more resources at it."

"Close it?" Beaumont asked.

"Summarize it. Leave it open on the official record for a while. Give the news hyenas time to find something else to howl about."

END

North Tower

Jerry and Beth hadn't planned to ride the subway together that morning. It just worked out that way. Beth was late for work and Jerry was going downtown to see about a job. They got off at Beth's station so Jerry could walk her to work. That was where they heard the noise.

Everybody on the underground platform heard the noise. It came from outside, high above, a sound like a giant beer can being crushed, blending immediately into a massive explosion. The shock wave reverberated into the subway and shook the air.

A hush fell over the crowd. A moment of stillness and palpable dread passed quickly. Movement resumed and chatter spread.

"The World Trade Center is on fire."

Jerry and Beth could move no faster than the crowd climbing the stairs. It was a few minutes before they got to the top and saw it was true.

Flames curled out of upper floor windows of one of the twin skyscrapers and licked up the outer walls. Clouds of smoke boiled out, billowing upward and trailing away in a long streamer. Smoldering debris fell, drifting this way and that on currents of superheated air, seeming to take forever to drop out of sight into the forest of surrounding buildings.

"It's the North Tower," Beth realized.

"Isn't that where you work?" Jerry asked.

"Yeah."

Beth was a waitress in an upper floor restaurant. She stood transfixed among the crowd, staring upward, and paid no attention to the strobes and deafening siren of a fire truck passing scant feet away on the street.

"It was an airplane," someone said. "The TV is saying an airplane hit the tower."

Down the street, close to the Trade Center block, people filtered out onto sidewalks. A trickle at first and then a growing rush that spilled out into the street. Many had no coats in spite of the September chill. The World Trade Center was under emergency evacuation.

Emergency vehicles filled the streets, threading their way through morning traffic. Police patrols on foot tried to move the gathering crowd back onto the sidewalk. People stared upward and ignored them.

Intense heat blew out windows in the floors above the fire in the North Tower. A figure appeared and jumped. The flutter of a dress revealed the jumper was a woman. She fell tumbling, taking what seemed forever to disappear behind an intervening building.

"That could have been you," Jerry realized.

The idea startled Beth visibly.

A cloud of dust and debris was forming at the base of the burning building and spreading outward. The sidewalk crowd began to retreat. Jerry shouldered people aside to make way for Beth.

"I'm sorry," Jerry said. "I shouldn't have said that."

"Maybe it was me," she said.

"Don't talk like that," Jerry said.

"No. Listen. I'm serious." She took his sleeve and tugged him to an empty doorway. "How much life insurance do we have?"

"What?"

"We have our own policy. I've got another one as a union benefit. I think they add up to twenty five thousand."

"You have to die to collect."

"The insurance company has to pay out if they believe you're dead."

"Whoa," Jerry said.

"We can do this," Beth insisted. "You go to the police and file a missing persons report. Tell them I was scheduled to work this shift in the North Tower."

"You didn't," Jerry said. "You were late."

"Look up there," Beth demanded, pointing up at the inferno raging in the North Tower. "Do you think anyone could survive that?"

"Probably not," Jerry admitted.

"The only people who know I didn't show up are gone. The records that prove I didn't clock in have burned in the fire."

"What happens when they find out you're not missing?"

"I've got some goofy girl friends. They've got this collective thing going up in Maine. I can crash there for a couple of months while you're doing the insurance claim. After that we can disappear to wherever we want."

"We'll get caught," Jerry said.

"By who?"

"The police. Faking an insurance claim is a crime."

"Jerry, the building is burning. You can feel the heat from here. There won't be any bodies left. The police won't know who was there and who wasn't."

"The insurance companies. They won't just pay. They'll check up. Ask questions."

"They're going to have hundreds of claims. Maybe thousands. Do you think anyone is going to notice a couple of nobodies like us? The world doesn't even know we exist."

"We could go to prison."

"For what? All you did was file a missing persons report when your wife didn't come home from work. That's what husbands are supposed to do."

"What about you?"

"What about me?"

"You ran away and hid."

Beth flashed an innocent smile. "If anyone ever finds out, I'll tell them I got shook up by what happened. I needed some alone time to pull myself together. There's no law against that. We can tell them the insurance claim was just a mix-up."

"It's still cheating," Jerry said.

"Who are we cheating? The insurance companies? Big corporations? They rip people like us off every day."

"That's just BS. Union talk."

"I feed their executives five days a week. I hear the conversations at the tables. All the schemes. All the bragging about the profits they're making."

"Those were your friends who died this morning," Jerry reminded her. "People you knew. People you worked with."

"They're gone," Beth said. "We can't help them. We're not taking anything away from them. Their families will get everything they're entitled to."

"It's not right."

Beth's voice hardened. "This is the real world. It's not like the Marine Corps. You can't just get in the chow line three times a day and somebody feeds you. You have to hustle."

Fate put an exclamation point at the end of her words. The roar of jet engines shook the air, growing louder. A swept-wing passenger jet appeared from just above the skyline, flying far too low for safe operation. It banked as it approached, until it was on a collision course with the South Tower of the World Trade Center.

The impact blew flame and debris through the building and out the other side. Even the crowd of jaded New Yorkers on the sidewalk where Jerry and Beth stood fell silent in horror.

Debris cascaded down, adding volume and velocity to the ground level cloud. The cloud advanced relentlessly, swallowing everything in its path. The sidewalk crowd was forced to retreat, collapsing on itself and growing denser and more fractious as it did.

The crowd's momentum carried Jerry and Beth with it. Beth had to keep a tight grip on Jerry's arm to keep from being knocked over. Jerry used his free arm to fend off people pushing around them.

"That was deliberate," Jerry said.

"What are you talking about?" Beth asked.

"The plane," Jerry said. "It was no accident what happened. You could tell someone flew that plane into the tower on purpose."

"Yeah. I saw."

"They must have known they were going to kill a lot of people."

"Enough already. I get it."

"Who would do something like that?"

"How would I know?"

Eventually the surge of the crowd abated. Jerry and Beth found refuge on a side street. They stood coughing the residue of dust out of their lungs.

"We should try to help," Jerry said when they had recovered a semblance of normal breathing.

"How?"

"There must be something we can do."

84

"Duty. Honor. Country. When are you going to grow up? What did you ever get from four years in the Marines?"

"I never asked for anything."

"Yeah. Right. You never asked for anything. You just let them kick you to the curb. And me along with you."

"We're getting by."

"Not any more, we're not. We're both out of work. If you didn't notice."

Beth was having no success trying to brush dust off her coat. Jerry made an effort to help, but it was hopeless.

"We'll find something else," he said. "We always have, haven't we?"

"Yeah. Right. If we're lucky we can get back to barely making ends meet. What about the kids we talked about having and won't ever be able to afford?"

"It'll work out. You'll see."

"How? We've got less than a hundred in the bank. How do we pay the rent? How long until we max out our credit cards?"

Jerry fidgeted, and Beth pounced.

"My big, brave husband and provider," she taunted. "We finally get our one chance at a decent pay day and he's too scared to take it."

"It's not about being scared," Jerry said.

"What is it about?"

"It's about doing the right thing," Jerry said. The insistence in his voice surprised him. "I guess you never really stop being a Marine."

"What about your big idea about going to college when you got out?" Beth demanded. "How many classes have you attended?"

"None. Yet"

"None ever," Beth corrected. "You're what, looking for your fifth job in two years?"

Jerry's shoulders sagged under the weight of failure.

Beth smiled and her voice softened. "You can't go through life just being one of the good guys."

"I'm not."

"Do you remember when you took me to the Senior Prom in high school?"

"Sure."

"We fucked afterward. It was your first time. You thought it meant you had to marry me."

All Jerry had to offer was an embarrassed grin.

"I thought I was doing better than all the other girls," Beth recalled fondly. "I was getting a big, handsome Marine."

"Yeah," was all Jerry said.

"We're not kids anymore," Beth said, and moved close to him. "All we've got is each other. That's all we'll ever have."

"I guess so," Jerry admitted.

"Things happen because they were meant to happen," Beth said.

The North Tower was engulfed flames by then, offering no hope of survival, just a great billow of smoke drifting into a miles-long cloud that darkened the city below. A belt of flames encircled the South Tower, just beginning its inevitable destruction. The strobes of first responders had vanished into the growing ground level cloud of dust and debris.

"Sure, this is a bad break for a lot of people," Beth said, "but maybe it was meant to happen for you and me."

"All those people" Jerry said quietly.

"They're with God," Beth assured him. "What was it Pastor Thomas said? They have done God's work on Earth, and now he has called them home."

Jerry had no answer for that.

"This is our chance," Beth said. "Our gift from God. We have to take it."

END

Harvest Time

"**H**i," Carl said to the woman on the barstool beside his. "My name is Geoff. What's yours?"

She didn't answer immediately. Dark, sultry eyes considered him with a sidelong look that he could feel between his legs.

"Indra," she finally said.

She was hooked.

The name validated Carl's guess that she was from South Asia. Her voice was as soft and pure as the chocolate skin of her face. She seemed to be teasing him with a minuscule smile that looked like it could be persuaded to be nicer if the right man said the right things. Cool and gorgeous and probably not a US Citizen. The perfect mark.

"What are you drinking?" he asked.

"Gin Gimlet."

She ran a forefinger around the rim of her glass, and then leaned close and gave him a head-spinning dose of perfume while she ran a forefinger slowly around the rim of his.

"I don't recognize yours," she said.

"Manhattan Cocktail. I'd like to buy you another, but it's pretty noisy here."

The bar was a meat market for young trendies. The place was crowded. Electronic music competed with the buzz of conversation.

"Maybe we could go someplace quiet," Carl suggested. "Someplace where we could talk. Get to know each other a little."

"I don't know," she said, and gave him a some more study.

Carl's smile was confident. Women liked his looks. He had kept up his gym time and his grooming.

"What do you do?" she asked. "For work, I mean."

Like maybe he wasn't good enough for her. Carl had an answer ready. "Law practice. Schroeder and Clift. Junior partner."

Okay, so what if he had flunked out of junior college years ago. Plenty of lawyers came into the foreign car dealership where he worked as a service consultant. He had watched them. Listened to how they talked. Studied how they dressed. Imitated how they acted. Rehearsed at home unto he could play the role to perfection. If the mark thought he was a lawyer, she was less likely to make trouble afterward. When she woke up and figured out what had happened.

Indra's smile came back. Still tentative, but it was back. Enough to tell Carl that the pitch was beginning to take hold. Time for the next step. Low key. Nice and easy.

"Seriously," he said, "I know a little place near here. Called the *Blue Note*. Jazz club. Upscale. Quiet. Three piece combo."

She nibbled her drink, stalling while she thought it over. "You're very sure of yourself, aren't you?"

"Force of habit," Carl said, plucking a snippet of conversation out of his memory. "There can't be any doubt in your mind when you present your case in court."

The look Indra gave him made Carl wonder if he had overdone it. He fortified himself with a drink from his Manhattan while he smiled at her over the glass with his eyes. No pressure. Let her think she was in control.

Women were freaks when it came to control. They had to feel like they had it, whether they did or not.

The two of them finished their drinks, Carl waiting patiently and pleasantly, Indra sizing him up.

"Why not," she decided.

Carl felt a flash of light-headedness when he stood up from the stool. Manhattan cocktails didn't usually hit him that way, but it was no big deal. Just a momentary flicker.

Maybe it was Indra. She was intoxicating in a way he had seldom felt. She was a study in grace swiveling off the bar stool. Her outfit suggested more than it revealed, but Carl couldn't help noticing the surreptitious glances she drew from men.

He was walking on air escorting her through the maze of tables to the door. He felt like telling the suckers with the hungry eyes to eat their hearts out.

Forget that. He had hit the mother lode. He had to focus on making his score.

The parking lot was full. Carl had lost track of where he left his car. He never did that. He had to think a minute before it dawned on him to use the key fob to blip the lights to locate it.

He had to fumble to get the key fob out of his pocket and then to get it right way round in his hand. He wasn't usually that clumsy. It took him a couple of tries to find the right button.

The car was a luxury sedan. Not quite new, but the kind of vehicle the up-and-coming executive types brought in for service. The payments took a serious bite out of the crummy salary the dealership paid him, but it was money he wouldn't have to throw away on endless dates with second-rate broads who were dreaming of finding some guy who was out of their league. All he needed was a ride that made the perfect impression.

Indra was impressed. She looked over the car and then gave Carl and admiring look. It was all going according to script.

Carl rehearsed the next steps in his mind while he walked Indra to the car. It would be a short drive to the *Blue Note*. Dim-lit basement club. Small, private tables. Perfect set up. Rick would install Indra at one of the tables and go for their drinks. When he got back, hers would have a roofie in it. Odorless. Tasteless. Invisible.

Then it would be light conversation. A little banter. Maybe another round of drinks. Pretty soon she wouldn't feel so good. He would look worried. Insist on driving her home. He had done the routine often enough to have it down pat.

She would be out cold when they got to the motel. Carry her into the room. It wouldn't be that hard. Even in heels she was a few inches shorter than he was. He had managed heavier women.

He was going to enjoy stripping her naked and spreading her out on the bed. He got hard just thinking about caressing her soft skin, having his way with no resistance.

Indra's perfume made him giddy when he held the car door for her.

A pulsating flicker of colored light dragged Carl out of the fog of sleep. The light was projected on flimsy window blinds from somewhere outside. After a minute he was able to make out letters of a neon motel sign.

He was on his back on an unfamiliar bed. He didn't recognize the room. He glanced around for anything that might jog his memory. Give him some clue where he was. How he had gotten there.

There was a chair a few feet away and his clothes were neatly folded on the seat. Something was wrong. He never folded his clothes.

A faintly medicinal smell permeated the room.

Carl was naked and he could feel something cold and hard at the small of his back. He felt numb and uncoordinated rolling to a sitting position. The something was a Ziploc bag filled with melting cubes of ice.

Carl's cell phone lay on the nightstand. Underneath was a computer printed message.

CALL 911 IMMEDIATELY
TELL THEM YOUR KIDNEYS HAVE BEEN REMOVED
THEY WILL KNOW WHAT TO DO

END

Heartbreak Hotel

I had never seen the guy before. He came in out of the night and the drizzle and stood looking around the narrow lobby, like maybe he expected a place to sit down.

There used to be a couple of wooden chairs. They had been wino magnets. They were gone now. There was nothing but the shadows too many years of sun had left when it faded the wallpaper around them.

The guy came to the registration desk.

"I'll take a room," he said.

He said it like he was used to giving orders, and having them followed right away.

"Twenty dollars," I said.

Usually it was twenty bucks, or just twenty, but this was the kind of guy you said dollars to. Close shave. Hair trimmed. Crisp smell of good liquor on his breath.

He fished in the side pocket of his suit coat and sorted out two fives and a ten from a wad of bills.

The suit hadn't come off any rack. I had a sport coat that had. The pockets on the sides of mine weren't pockets. Just flaps, so it looked like you had pockets. This guy's threads were custom made. Even with the rain spots, they said money.

The guy scribbled something in the register. For all I knew it was his real name. He took his key and he went up the stairs. Maybe he didn't see the elevator. Maybe he just wanted exercise. It was nothing to me. I put in my ear-buds and went back to reading.

MP3 player, you had your own jukebox. E-reader, you had your own library. It wasn't much, but it was what I had in life. You hang on to what you got. Make the best of it.

Right now I had the night. I had the quiet. I had some time to myself.

A few cars swished by outside, throwing light through the street window. There was a nightclub three blocks down, but it would be hours before it drew any sirens or police strobes.

The neon light flickered over the pawnshop across the street. The old Jew turned it out every night when he closed up, but there was something wrong with the switch. Sometimes it started flickering after he was gone. It always spooked me. Like it was alive and it knew something I didn't.

Headlights on the street washed out the neon and there was the brief rumble of an engine out at the curb. Then the headlights and the rumble were gone. I knew what to expect.

The man was short, black. A dapper little number. He strutted in wearing a gray fedora and a charcoal vest over a bright yellow silk shirt.

He made a production of holding the door for a woman.

She was Asian. Older than he was by a few years. Living on the tail end of some pretty good looks.

They came over and the black tapped two fingers on the desk.

"We will have a room, my man."

"Forty bucks," I said.

The woman gave me a look. "The sign outside says twenty."

There was a little fog of liquor in her eyes, but her words were crystal clear. Her coat said money, without screaming it. Her pearl drop earrings were all class, no flash.

"Twenty dollars single occupancy," I said. "Forty dollars double occupancy."

That surprised her, like she knew how ritzy hotel chains priced their rooms. Before she could give me an argument, the black took out a wallet and counted down two twenties. It was culture, I guess. One wanted to dicker. The other wanted to show off.

I turned to get a key and when I turned back the woman was staring at the stairs.

"Jack?"

The guy I had checked in earlier was standing there, looking back at her and not smiling.

"This the bottom, Mona?" he asked. "Or have you still got a ways to fall?"

"You son of a bitch."

Maybe three good steps separated them. The lobby was that small. She looked ready to charge across and tear into him.

"You followed me," she said. "Like some goddamn stalker."

"Do you really think you're worth that much effort?" he asked in a casual voice that didn't go with the hard set of his features.

"You're here, aren't you?"

"Nothing to it. You're in a committed relationship with your cell. I popped your number into the find my phone app. Where there's a sleazy nightclub, there's a cheap hotel not far off. Took me thirty seconds to think of it and thirty minutes to drive here. And I'm no more than half sober."

The guy named Jack hadn't wanted a room. Just an excuse to stand out of sight up the stairs and wait for Mona.

The dapper little black saw his evening going south and stepped between the two of them. He faced Jack, drawn up to his full five and a half feet.

"Look here, brother man," he began, and flicked open a knife.

The knife was long and slim, the blade sharp and shiny. He held the ivory handle lightly in his fingers, waving the blade in front of Jack's face slowly and hypnotically, like the head of a cobra.

"You shouldn't be talking to this fine lady like--."

I didn't know if Jack was naturally fast or if his move was so unexpected it was just startling. He snatched the knife out of the black's fingers and shoved him aside to confront Mona.

I went cold inside.

This wasn't just a domestic spat any more. It was an angry man carrying a load of liquor and an open knife.

"Well?" he demanded.

"Well what?" she shot back.

"You've got nothing to say for yourself?"

"What would be the point? You don't hear anything I say. You never have. You never will."

"I heard you all those years ago," he said.

His voice was suddenly quiet and bitter.

"All that talk about wanting something permanent. Marriage. Home. Family and--"

"Lonely nights," she interrupted, taking on the same bitter tone. "Excuses. Business trips."

"You think it's free? The exclusive neighborhood. The center hall colonial you just had to have. The private boarding schools."

They stood staring at each other. It sounded like an old argument. One that had been going on for a long time. One that was boiling up to the point that words wouldn't be enough anymore.

The little black dude was trapped in a corner. His fedora was crooked. His bravado was gone. He looked like an animal at bay. I had no idea what other weapons he had. Or what craziness might be running around in his head.

Jack had forgotten the little man existed. He smiled at Mona. A small gesture, tight and sarcastic.

"This time I made an effort," he said. "Cut the trip short so I could surprise you. Only I got the surprise. Empty house. No Mona."

"And that was your cue to do a half-gainer into a bottle of single malt?" she asked.

It sounded like my cue to say something.

"Look, folks," I began.

They didn't hear it. I could hardly hear it. It wasn't words, just a scared croak.

"I made an effort," Jack repeated.

His voice was getting louder. Tendons in his neck strained the collar of his shirt. There were tremors in the hand that held the knife.

"One night," she said.

I could see tears in her eyes. I put together all the nerve I could find and spoke up.

"Maybe this isn't the best place for--."

"One night!" she screamed. "After all these years!"

She lashed out and ripped his cheek open with her fingernails. The knife came up.

Crap.

I should have called 911 when it started. I fumbled for the phone and knocked it off the desk. It hit the floor with a clatter.

The noise startled Jack. He stared at me like he had forgotten I existed. He looked at the knife in his hand, like he couldn't remember where he got it. Like he wasn't sure what to do with it.

Mona realized where she was. She felt the tears running down her cheeks and tried to brush them away. Her eyes were fixed on Jack. Like she was too embarrassed to look anywhere else. Her mouth worked a couple of times before she found her voice.

"Do--do you want to go home?" she asked.

I think Jack said, "Yeah."

I couldn't really tell. That's how quiet his voice was. The tension was gone. He folded the knife and dropped it into his pocket.

"I guess so," he said.

He sounded like the liquor was dying inside him.

They left together. She had a handkerchief out, wiping the blood from his cheek.

The black dude was probably entitled to his forty bucks back. He never asked for it. Just straightened his fedora and squared his little shoulders.

"I didn't have my shit on me," he explained solemnly.

I just nodded.

"Ain't nobody does me like that when I got my shit on me."

He strutted out and drove away.

I guess that's how it was. You hung on to what you had in life. It didn't matter how tarnished it got. It was what you had. You made the best of it.

Across the street the pawnbroker's neon flickered out.

END

Risk Management

i

The elevator door opened and Cilla pushed her cleaning cart through the lobby onto the deserted trading floor. The trading floors were her favorites. Her nightly cleaning routine of dusting and vacuuming and emptying was tightly scheduled. It gave her no time to gaze out the windows of the office skyscraper at the pulsing lights and nocturnal bustle of the city forty odd stories below. The desktop computers and the Bloomberg machines made up for that.

Cilla didn't know what a Bloomberg machine was for, except that it had something to do with stocks and bonds. She just knew that the dancing patterns of tiny numbers and colors and the friendly screen savers on the computers were signs of life that brightened a lonely shift and eased the relentless nagging of arthritis.

She was surprised when she heard an elevator door open. After a minute fluorescent lights came on in an office at the far end of the floor. A few more people arrived. The last was a tall man with flat shoulders tailored into an expensive suit. Only the absence of a tie made him seem slightly less formal and important. He paused, fished in his pockets, put a tiny spoon under his nose and inhaled. Then he squared his shoulders and marched into the lighted office without bothering to close the door.

His voice carried clearly and forcefully. "I apologize for the late hour, but this is an all-hands-on-deck situation. As you are all aware. the firm deals extensively in mortgage-backed securities. We are critically short of the mortgage instruments we need to properly layer those securities. The top floor wants that situation corrected. That starts with us, at the opening bell tomorrow."

The next voice belonged to a woman. "We've been looking. High quality mortgage packages are getting harder to find."

"No excuses. I want your teams to hit every source. Track down every lead. Turn over every rock. Buy every mortgage package they can find."

Another voice. A man this time. He sounded worried. "The mortgage component is supposed to mitigate the risk of our securities. The adjustable rate product we're seeing now is risky all by itself."

"Forget the college boy crap. We're traders. We buy and sell. That's what we do. That's how we earn our living. That's how we make our bonus numbers. Let the big brains upstairs worry about risk. I want every team and every trader laser focused."

The office emptied out and the elevators took the traders away. Cilla was left with the flicker of friendly screens and the security of a scheduled cleaning routine. She couldn't shake the memory of the conversation. She didn't understand financial things. She knew she never would. But people who did understand them sounded worried.

ii

Sunday was Cilla's favorite day of the week. She would go to Mass with her son and daughter-in-law, Moira, and help keep the grandchildren from fidgeting. The grandchildren were a joy. Their energy and excitement brightened the whole day. Cilla would go home with the family and help with lunch and spend the afternoon.

"I'm sorry Jamie couldn't go today," Moira said while she and Cilla were making sandwiches. "He has to work two jobs now. The mortgage payment went up again, and it's been so hard to meet all the expenses."

"Sometimes we just have to have faith that everything will turn out," Cilla said.

She wished she could do something to help, but she earned only enough to keep herself from being a burden to the family.

"The Lord will watch over us and see that everything turns out."

Cilla wanted to believe, but sometimes the words sounded hollow. It was worse when the grandchildren asked why the family couldn't adopt a kitten. It wasn't right to have to tell children to be patient and wait. They would only be young once.

iii

Cilla knew something had happened on the trading floors during the day. They were her floors. She was responsible for them and she was proud of that responsibility. She knew every aisle and every desk. They didn't look the same tonight.

Some of the desks were empty. Not a lot, but they were obvious, like the gaps made by missing teeth. Screens were dark and desk surfaces that had held personal items and family photos were bare. A few folded cardboard bankers' boxes bore witness to what had happened, and to the fact that people would never be coming back.

Cilla dutifully scrubbed down the bare surfaces and checked to make sure the drawers had been emptied. It was part of the cleaning routine, but her heart wasn't in it. She remembered the family photos. The happy faces of the children. What would happen to the smiles when there was no job to support them and put food on the table.

Weeks passed into months, and there were more empty desks. The television news talked about an epidemic of mortgage foreclosures. Cilla didn't understand exactly how the two were connected, but she knew they were in some far-off, mysterious way.

iv

Moira was crying when she phoned. It wasn't tears spilling over from a marital spat. These were racking sobs, strong enough that she was hardly able to get a few words out. It took Cilla a minute to realize her son and daughter in law were going to lose their home.

"The mortgage payment was adjusted," Moira said. "It went up so high. Twice what it was, the payment. We go to the bank and ask why and they say it is in the contract. The interest rate is adjusted up to market."

Cilla had heard the stories on the television news. She couldn't believe it was happening to her family.

"We ask the bank if there is something they can do," Moira said, "but they say no. They just administer the contract. They already sold the mortgage to a financing company to get money to write other mortgages."

Cilla's heart sank. The traders on the floors she cleaned had worried about the risk of adjustable rate mortgages. Now the worry was real and intensely personal.

"We tried to pay," Moira said. "Maybe if we can save up and make every other payment we can catch up later. But it is no good. The foreclosure notice came today."

v

Cilla knew something was wrong when she reported for work. She knew as soon as she stepped into the basement room where the cleaning carts were kept. Some of the night crew were already gathered there. Others were filtering in. There was no noisy bustle. None of the usual coming and going. No one said anything.

A large man in a suit stood with the shift supervisor. No one in a suit ever came here. The shift supervisor introduced him as Mr. Arkebauer. He was an executive in the company that managed the building.

Mr. Arkebauer's voice was as solemn as Father McNeil saying Mass.

"As some of you may know from watching the news on television, the nation's financial crisis has come to a head. The Federal Government has had to intervene. The banks and brokerage houses that rent space in this building are working through a difficult time. Now they will either be downsizing or winding up their business entirely. As a result, they will no longer require the space they currently occupy in the building. This means that a considerable number of floors, in fact well more than half the building, will no longer require nightly cleaning."

Dead silence. Everyone in the room knew what was coming, and no one knew what to say. Mr. Arkebauer went on quickly.

"This is not anyone's fault. You have all done an admirable job. Each and every one of you can be proud of the work you have done, and of the service you have rendered to the financial community and the building tenants. On behalf of the management, let me thank you for your years of dedication and assure you that your efforts have not gone unnoticed or unappreciated. Unfortunately, events beyond anyone's control compel the management to take action that no one wanted."

vi

Cilla took her cleaning cart up to her floors for the last time. They told her she was one of the lucky ones. She had enough seniority to retire. She would have her union pension and health insurance. Most of the others on the night crew would have to hope that enough floors in the building would be leased soon and occupied quickly so they could be re-hired.

Cilla didn't feel lucky. These floors had been her life for more than ten years. She had come here nights when she was sick because it was her duty. She endured the pain of arthritis because this was her opportunity to be useful, to make whatever little contribution she was able to make in the world. That would all be gone in a few fleeting hours.

She hardly recognized the first of her floors. The walls had been stripped of artwork. The cheerful pictures she had dusted were just dark rectangles on the sun bleached plasterboard. Some of the desks were already gone. Aisle-ways had been dismantled and sound absorbing panels stacked against one wall. The floor beneath was bare carpet broken only by the aluminum humps of electrical outlets. She knew that her world was gone.

Her instructions were simple. Normal cleaning for the elevator lobby and any areas still occupied. Vacuum any remaining carpet. Ignore areas where moving or demolition had occurred. Her heart wasn't in it. She wanted to remember her floors as she had left them for so many years. Bright and spotless and ready for the next day.

Cilla had seen the video on the television news. The tents and the outdoor kitchens and the big banner that read *Occupy Wall Street*. This was the first time she had seen it for herself, and it looked empty and lifeless by comparison.

It was a weekday morning and she had ridden the subway downtown to sign the papers that would officially begin her new life. There was drizzle in the air. Gusts of chilly wind had cleared the sidewalks of all but a random straggle of pedestrians. A few protesters were huddled where they could find shelter, signs propped against walls, talking among themselves.

Cilla didn't understand what they expected to gain protesting. She understood that greed had upended lives. It had upended hers, and left her family struggling, but she didn't see any point in complaining, or anything to demand. The greedy had paid with their careers, and left only empty buildings to testify to their failure. There didn't seem to be anything else they could forfeit.

The protesters said they wanted change, but it didn't seem reasonable to change from the system that had built the skyscrapers that still rose majestically above the street and had once offered jobs and pride to people like her. She hoped in her heart that it would all come back eventually. And that everyone would be wiser and stronger for enduring the pain. She had never asked that life be easy or fair. Just that there would be a place for her.

END

Feeding Frenzy

i

Bennie was fidgeting aimlessly in the back row of English class when the policeman came in and called his name.

The other kids turned and stared at him. He was confused. He hated being stared at and he felt his face turning red.

The policeman put a huge paw around his arm and hauled him out of his desk. The officer didn't say anything, just collected Bennie's backpack, took him out and seatbelted him in a police SUV. The back seat was surrounded by metal screening. It smelled bad.

The Police Station was a scary glass and steel building on the grassy campus of a suburban civic center. The policeman took Bennie inside and deposited him in a small room with no windows. There were plastic chairs and a small table.

"Sit here and wait." The policeman closed the door when he left.

Bennie needed to pee.

It seemed like a long time until his mom came. She was still dressed for work. Her eyes were frantic.

"Bennie, what happened?"

"I don't know. A policeman came to school."

"The police are searching the house. What did you do?"

Bennie hated it when his mom blamed him for things, but he knew the best could do was just shake his head.

The detective who came in announced that his name was Krieghoff.

He was overweight and balding. His shirt sleeves were turned back over thick, hairy forearms. He settled importantly in a chair across the small table from Bennie and his mom.

"When did Caleb Carson first talk about going to the mall and shooting people?" he asked.

Caleb Carson lived down the street from Bennie and his mom. He was small and nervous and scary. Bennie didn't know him except to say hello.

Bennie's mom was stunned. "Did you know this was going to happen?"

"What?" Bennie asked.

"People were shot at a mall. All the TV stations have pre-empted their regular programming."

Bennie had been in school all day. They didn't let you watch TV in school. Detective Krieghoff didn't give him a chance to speak.

"When was the last time you talked to Caleb Carson?"

"I didn't."

It was a stupid question. Caleb was a senior. Seniors didn't hang out with ninth graders like Bennie. Everyone knew that.

Before Krieghoff could say anything more, the door opened and a woman stepped in. She was tall and angular, well dressed. Krieghoff didn't seem to recognize her.

"My name is Ardella Hawkins," she informed him. "I will be providing legal counsel for Bennie and his mother. My bar number and contact information are on file at the desk, but I will be happy to repeat them for your audio-video surveillance."

ii

Ardella Hawkins closed the door with a sharp click. "I would like to know the charges and probable cause for Bennie's detention."

"We are investigating circumstances surrounding this morning's mall shooting. Bennie had recent correspondence with the deceased shooter, Caleb Carson."

"The nature of the correspondence?"

Krieghoff put a sheet of paper on the table.

Hey, dude, I'm putting my life on the line for this neighborhood. They're watching me. I know they are. You got to tell me if you see strange people.

It was a printout of an e-mail Bennie vaguely remembered deleting.

"Bennie's response?" Ardella Hawkins demanded.

"We are working to determine that now."

"This is merely a solicitation for exchange of e-mail. If there was no response, there was no correspondence."

Krieghoff held his tongue.

"My clients are terminating this interview."

"Ms Hawkins, this is a serious matter. We need to establish the facts to ensure there is no ongoing threat to public safety."

"Probable cause to detain?" Ardella Hawkins repeated.

Bennie was released to the custody of his mom.

iii

Bennie's mom lectured during the drive home, but Bennie didn't really listen. It was stuff about how he should have told her about getting e-mail from Caleb Carson. She was going to close his e-mail account as soon as the police gave her back the computer. She was going to take away his phone, as soon as the police gave that back.

The police had his backpack. His school notebooks were inside. Maybe they would think there was something wrong with him mentally when they read the little scribbles he sometimes made in the margins. It just didn't seem fair. He never did anything to hurt anyone.

Bennie had always felt secure on the quiet street where he and his mom lived. No more. There were police SUVs and a big white van that said *Police Evidence Unit*. Television news trucks with big antenna dishes on top lurked like scavengers just outside the police tape around the Carson house.

There were no familiar neighbors anywhere in sight. It was like one of those science fiction movies where an army of aliens invaded and scared everyone into their homes.

Bennie's mom called his dad and told him to come over after dinner. That meant Bennie would have to go to his room. He always had to go to his room when his mom and dad argued, even back when they were still married. It didn't really matter. Bennie could hear everything through the door.

iv

"The police took Bennie out of school," his mom said. "I had to hire a lawyer."

"What lawyer?" Bennie's dad wanted to know.

"Ardella Hawkins."

"The woman is a communist."

"She has championed progressive causes."

"She hates the police."

"She isn't afraid of them."

"She costs an arm and a leg," Bennie's dad said. "All those big name lawyers do. I'm not paying a dime of it."

"The TV station called. They wanted an interview. They offered to pay."

"Yeah. Right. To juice their ratings. The news media are the ones who cause all these shootings. Do you think the crazies would pull this crap if they didn't know they'd be the lead story on national television?"

"What about Bennie?" his mom asked.

"He didn't do anything, did he?"

"He says he doesn't know anything about it."

Bennie cringed. He knew from his mom's tone of voice that she didn't believe him. She never believed men or boys. Maybe if he'd been a girl.

"We all keep our heads down and let it blow over," his dad said. "There's nothing else we can do. This is a gold mine. Everyone is going to be looking to get a piece of the action. The politicians. The cops. Media. Lawyers. Counselors. They're going to milk it for all it's worth."

vi

Bennie had to see a counselor before he was allowed to go back to school. Nobody said why exactly, except to make a big deal out of telling him that he wasn't being punished.

Bennie had to wait in the reception area while his mom talked to the counselor. She came out with the same expectant look she got when she was nagging him to try out for some stupid sports team.

"You'll like Mrs. Thomas, Bennie. She's very nice. She's going to help you."

Mrs. Thomas was a pale woman who sat behind a shiny black and chromium desk and greeted him with dark, probing eyes.

"Come in, Bennie."

She offered a reassuring smile and revealed an expensive wedding set when she used a hand to indicate a chair in front of the desk.

"Please sit down and be comfortable."

Bennie didn't feel comfortable. The office had a big plant in the corner. It looked hungry. The art on the walls was modern and alien. There was a weird clock on the desk. Bennie could see right through it. The second hand turned even though there were no visible workings inside.

The chair was a black leather and chromium snare waiting for its next victim. Bennie sat uncertainly at the front edge of the cushion.

"Bennie, I'm here to help you understand some of your feelings."

Bennie didn't know what she expected him to say.

"Things you might have felt watching the television news for example," she said.

"I'm not allowed to watch TV."

Bennie's mom had taken away his TV privileges, so he could only turn on the news when she was away at work. There was a lot about the mall shooting. News people all dressed up and trying to look important with big monitors flashing behind them. Politicians in suits and police in their fanciest uniforms talking to the cameras. People being interviewed saying how awful it was.

It didn't mean much to Bennie. He had seen the same stuff on TV lots of times. He didn't know any of the people in the pictures they showed. He didn't recognize the mall. He had never even been there.

"Do you feel safe at school?" Mrs. Thomas asked.

"Yeah." Why wouldn't he?

"Do you have many friends at school?"

Bennie knew where that came from. His mom was always nagging him to make more friends. To be popular. To be a leader in school. He just shrugged.

"Are you lonely?" Mrs. Thomas asked. "Is that why you became friends with Caleb Carson?"

"I didn't know him."

"Bennie, do you know what denial is?"

That didn't sound good, like maybe he was about to be blamed for something again. Bennie didn't say anything.

"Denial is when something traumatic happens in our lives, something difficult to deal with, and we try to push it out of our minds. We try to pretend it didn't really happen."

Bennie fidgeted at the edge of the chair cushion. Mrs. Thomas had made up her mind that he was a head case. There was nothing he could do about it.

"Sometimes we have to accept that bad things have happened," Mrs. Thomas said. "The best thing we can do is talk about them."

Bennie sat silent. There was no point arguing with adults. Once they got something in their minds, that was it. The only thing to do was let them lecture. Eventually they would get tired and give up. His mom called it being impossible.

vii

Mr. Pritchard was the District Attorney. Bennie had seen him talking to a bank of microphones on TV. He looked smaller and more threatening sitting behind a big desk and peering through the lenses of rimless glasses.

Bennie sat in front of the desk. His mom sat on one side and Ardella Hawkins on the other, but Mr. Pritchard was lecturing Bennie.

"It is important that we learn where Caleb Carson got the rifle he used."

Bennie tried not to squirm.

"What did Caleb tell you about that?" Mr. Pritchard asked.

"I never talked to him."

"Bennie, do you know it is crime to withhold information about a crime?"

"My client," Ardella Hawkins interrupted, "denies having the information. What evidence does the State have to the contrary?"

"According to the counselor, Bennie is a very withdrawn boy," Mr. Pritchard said. "He may well be experiencing denial."

"Intuition is not evidence," Ardella Hawkins shot back.

"This is the professional opinion of a licensed, court approved practitioner."

"Counseling is a for-profit enterprise. Any finding that indicates further treatment is an opportunity for ongoing revenue."

"It is imperative that we learn where the rifle was sourced," Mr. Pritchard insisted.

"You cannot blame a minor child for the investigative shortcomings of the civil authorities."

Bennie quit listening. They weren't arguing about him. They were arguing because they didn't like each other.

Bennie was nervous when he went back to school on Monday, but nobody stared at him. Two girls had been caught smoking marijuana in the locker room. That's all the kids were talking about. Bennie didn't even exist.

END

Skid Row

"**H**er name is Mindy."

The woman's hand trembled when she held out the photograph. She was younger than Grace by perhaps ten years. At forty-something her once attractive face had gown careworn. There was an uncertain throb of hope in her voice.

"I thought you might have seen her."

The photograph was a professional eight by ten portrait. The subject was a cheerful girl in her mid-teens, dressed up for the occasion.

"No, I'm sorry," Grace said gently. "I haven't."

"On Skid Row," the woman said. "They told me you were one of the ladies who volunteered with the church. That you went once a week and talked to the people who camped on the sidewalk there. I thought you might have seen her."

"No. I haven't."

"We've tried everything." The woman's eyes pleaded for understanding. "Clinics. Doctors. Intervention. She always goes back to the drugs."

"You mustn't give up," Grace said.

She couldn't help the cheerful girl in the photograph, but she didn't want to think of her alone and abandoned. Her mother's resolve was sliding into desperation, and hanging on by a thread.

"If I could just find her. If I knew where she was. Will you take her picture and look? I've written my phone number and address on the back."

Grace put the picture in her binder and sent the woman on her way with what little reassurance she could offer.

There was no time for sympathy. Grace had more blocks than usual to cover. Reverend Sherman was in the hospital with an infected rat bite. They said he might lose part of one leg.

Grace laced her army paratroop boots tight to shield her ankles and secured the cuffs of her trouser legs over the protective leather with bicycle clips. A heavy jacket with a clip-on ID and latex gloves and she was ready to catch the bus for her weekly sojourn.

On her way out she stopped for a look at the tall crucifix behind the altar.

"Lord," she whispered, "grant me the courage to change what I can, the serenity to accept what I cannot and the wisdom to know the difference."

Grace knew when the smell first hit her that she would need all the strength she could muster. It was a warm morning and the heat made the stench of rotting garbage and human waste worse. She was already sweating inside her jacket, but she kept it zipped tight. There was no telling what she might come in contact with as she threaded through the welter of tents along the sidewalk.

Disappointment was quick in coming.

Mary was back where Grace had first found her. A month of patient conversation had drawn out that she was a member of an indigenous tribe from the northern part of the state. The indigenous were good about looking after their own. Grace had contacted the Tribal Council and they had come and collected Mary.

Now she was back, sitting cross legged and defiant on her tiny patch of sidewalk.

"Nope," she announced. "Ain't going."

Argument would carry no weight against fierce independence. It was a small victory that Mary remembered who Grace was.

"Will you tell me why not?" Grace asked to see if she could build on that"

"Ain't going. Don't wanna."

There was no emotion, no eye contact. Just a stout, stolid woman who had retreated into a world of her own. Grace made a note to call the Tribal Council. At least that way Mary's people would know where she was.

Grace navigated a block of closed up tents.

At first she didn't see the ragged old man. He was hunched into a corner made by a retaining wall and a concrete support pillar, shivering in the heat.

"Sir, are you all right."

"Lemme be," the man whined.

He tried to squeeze deeper into his corner, but there was no room. The movement shifted his threadbare jeans and exposed patches of red skin on his bony shins.

"Do you need medical attention?" Grace asked.

"Lemme be."

"Sir, your legs are infected."

"Them's just wine sores. That's all. Lemme be."

He pulled a flimsy jacket tighter around him. There was something underneath the jacket.

"I won't touch your bottle," Grace promised.

"Thunder chicken." A smile of anticipation exposed missing teeth. "Mighty good lickin'."

"There is a free clinic near here. I can walk with you."

"Lemme be. Just lemme be."

There was nothing else to do.

Another block of closed up tents. Ragged sheets of plywood with filthy epithets spray painted. Garbage, scurrying rats and discarded needles. One of the volunteer doctors had called it medieval squalor.

The man who stepped in front of Grace intended to startle her. He was tall and broad and heavily bearded. Tattoos on both burly arms suggested time in prison.

"Gimme twenty bucks," he demanded.

He must be desperate to confront her here. There was police activity visible in the next block. Grace didn't carry cash. All she had to offer was a smile.

"Do you want the money for drugs?" she asked.

"Gimme twenty bucks."

His voice was louder, angrier. Grace did what she could to control her fear. She spoke quietly to try to calm the man.

"I can give you a referral to treatment. They understand how difficult it can be to deal with the cravings. The service won't cost anything.

Frustration welled up in the man's eyes and boiled out in his voice. "Gimme twenty bucks, you stupid bitch."

Grace was no longer listening. Something down the street had caught her eye. Paramdics were steering a gurney through the maze of tents toward the rear of a fire department medical truck. The casualty had barely enough to bulk to disturb the lay of the covering blanket. The blanket was drawn all the way over the victim, and the paramedics were in no hurry.

Grace had to reach them before they loaded the gurney and were gone. Not because of anything she knew, but because of what she feared.

The man confronting her was accustomed to terrorizing his prey. He wasn't ready for the sudden movement of a woman full of purpose. Grace stepped around him and started down the sidewalk at the fastest walk she could safely manage.

"Gimme twenty bucks," he called helplessly after her.

The sidewalk was a minefield of litter, and heedless traffic made venturing out into the street too dangerous. Grace wanted to call out to the paramedics to stop, to wait, but it took all her concentration to pick her way through the debris.

Grace reached the gurney just as the paramedics were preparing to load it into the back of the fire department truck. She drew the blanket back from the victim's face.

It was the face of a young woman, gaunt and lined beyond her years. Livid color was creeping into the pallor of her skin, a sign of death some hours old. Grace's heart sank.

"Here, what are you doing?"

It was the authoritative voice of a black woman, not tall but powerfully built. Sergeant's stripes on the sleeve of her police uniform made her the incident supervisor. She looked at the ID tag clipped to Grace's jacket.

"You know better than that. This girl is entitled to a little dignity."

"Her name is Mindy," Grace said sadly. "I have her mother's contact information."

She took the photograph out of her binder and handed it over. The Sergeant compared the cheerful girl in the picture with the haggard face on the gurney. It took a minute for her to satisfy herself.

"All right," she said, and nodded for the paramedics to load the body.

"I can call her mother," Grace offered.

"Our job now," the Sergeant said. "That and arranging for formal identification."

Grace could only imagine the mother's grief when she had to view her daughter's remains in the morgue. At least she wouldn't have to see the awful place where Mindy died. There was a time when Grace wondered how Skid Row could exist in a city as wealthy as Los Angeles. It wasn't until she came and walked the streets that she realized how difficult it was to make even the slightest difference.

The first responders did what they could on their all-too-frequent calls, but that was like trying to cure cancer with a band-aid. The Sergeant clipped the photograph to the back of her tablet.

"We'll be leaving soon. There is a bus coming. You had better get on it."

The Sergeant was right, of course. The police were hated on Skid Row. That hatred extended to anyone who talked to them. Next week all memory of today would have vanished in the fog of alcohol and drugs, and it would be safe for Grace to come back. For now it was too dangerous to continue.

Grace boarded the bus and took a window seat where she could watch it all scroll past. Endless blocks of sidewalk encampment. People making their perilous way from one day to the next in poverty and filth. The inevitable death sentences foreshadowed by discarded needles.

Grace dreaded the day she might come face-to-face with a drug overdose. She wasn't allowed to carry Narcon. She was only allowed to talk to people. Physical interdiction in the midst of a potentially hostile population was too dangerous. Reverend Sherman was adamant. The tools of the Lord were faith and compassion, and they were wielded with patience, not force.

It was tempting to think the hand of God had guided her to Mindy. That she had been able to bring an end to her poor mother' anxiety. The situation would never turn out well. There was an element of mercy in a quick resolution. A chance to begin the healing process.

Grace wanted that to be true. She could summon the courage to change what she could. The serenity to accept what she could not was a much heavier lift.

Her friends had no end of questions.

Why did she volunteer?

What did she think she could accomplish?

Those people chose to live the way they did. Why not let them?

Did she think she could hold back the tide?

The fact that she couldn't do everything didn't mean she shouldn't do anything. Miracles were the province of God. All she asked was that she be allowed to make her small contribution when she could. And to bear witness when she couldn't.

END

School Daze

The woman ensconced behind the desk was somewhere past fifty. A colorful scarf tried to soften the authority of her business suit. Her smile tried to project maternal warmth. Neither succeeded.

"Mei Lin Feng?" she asked.

"Fung," Mei Lin corrected.

"Excuse me?"

"My last name," Mei Lin said. "It's spelled Feng but it's pronounced Fung."

"Do sit down."

At twenty one Mei Lin was petite and pleasant, quietly dressed. She seated herself demurely in front of the desk. Her posture was stiff enough to betray nerves.

"I am Mrs. Detweiler," the woman said. "I am a senior counselor with the office of the State Superintendent of Education."

Mei Lin smiled. She didn't seem to know what else to do.

"I want to assure you this interview will be held in strict confidence," Mrs. Detweiler said. "You are encouraged to speak freely."

Mei Lin limited herself to a cautious nod.

Mrs. Detweiler consulted a slim line laptop. "You attended Benjamin Franklin High School before you came here to the university?"

"Yes."

"Did the other students at Franklin have trouble pronouncing your last name correctly?"

"Everyone called me Muffie. I mean all my friends."

"Tell me about your school friends."

"What about them?"

"Who were they? The ones you were closest to."

Mei Lin smiled at the memory. "Nickels. T-Bone. Mudrock. Sharkey."

"Were they male or female, or a mixture of genders?"

"Nicolette Stevenson. Teresa Bonner. Evelyn Murdock. Sharon Keys."

"Did they all identify as female?"

"Yes." The question surprised Mei Lin.

"Were they a diverse group? Mixed ethnicity?"

"They were white. Caucasian."

"How did you get to know them?"

"We all grew up a couple of blocks apart. We walked to school together since forever. We were the D Street Crew."

"Have you kept in touch since high school?"

"Not so much," Mei Lin said with a touch of regret.

"Why not?"

"Nickels killed the National Merit. She got a partial ride to Stanford. T-Bone has two little ones and no time for anything else. Mudrock is on the road selling pharma. Sharkey is a senior over at Moo U."

Mrs. Detweiler considered Mei Lin with the detached scrutiny 0f a scientist examining a laboratory specimen.

"Does it trouble you that a Caucasian like Nicolette Stevenson received a National Merit Scholarship when you didn't?"

"No." Mei Lin bristled at the suggestion. "We all took the same test. Nickels outscored everyone else. Good for her."

Mrs. Detweiler consulted her computer again. "You did quite well in your course work at Franklin. You had mostly As. But you did receive consistent Bs in Physical Education."

"Yeah. Yes."

"You appear quite athletic. Like you might excel at sports. Did you feel you were fairly graded in physical education?"

"Yeah. Yes."

"Did you play sports in school?"

"My parents signed me up for junior golf. That's the only sport I was ever really interested in."

"Did you try out for the university team?"

"No."

"Did you feel you might be discriminated against because of your Asian ethnicity?"

"Because of my eight handicap. This is a division one school. The girls on the team are scholarship players. They are recruited from all over the country. From Europe and Korea. Most of them shoot scratch or better."

It was a good answer with a firm foundation in fact and it left Mei Lin visibly relaxed and confident. It wasn't what Mrs. Detweiler wanted to hear. She went back to her laptop for more ammunition.

"You also took Spanish as a high school elective."

"Yes."

"Why did you elect Spanish."

"I heard people speak it. In stores and on the bus and places. I was curious to know what they were saying."

"Was that because you felt an affinity with other people of color?"

"No. I'm just snoopy." Mrs. Detweiler smiled to stifle frustration. Her efforts to build rapport and guide the conversation were going nowhere.

"Do you know why this interview is being conducted?"

"No. I just got an e-mail from the college that told me when to be here."

"There was a fight in the girl's locker room during your senior year at Franklin High. One of the students had a knife. Do you remember how you felt when you heard about that?"

Mei Lin was blank. "I never heard about anything like that."

Disbelief put a crisp edge on Mrs. Detweiler's voice. "Other students must have talked about it."

"The only fights the kids at school talked about were the ones in the parking lot at *Choosy's*."

"It was in the newspapers. It received television coverage."

"My parents were big into the news. I never paid much attention."

"Lawsuits have been working their way through the courts," Mrs. Detweiler informed her. "They were resolved recently with a consent decree. The State Superintendent of Education has been tasked with devising and overseeing a program to build a more supportive and inclusive atmosphere at Benjamin Franklin High School. We are interviewing former students to learn whether they have suggestions for improvement."

"Oh, yeah," Mei Lin said. "Yes. Definitely."

Mrs. Detweiler smiled expectantly and moved her laptop for convenient typing.

"More advanced classes," Mei Lin said. "When I got to university all I had for math was algebra and trig. Some of the guys majoring in software engineering had introductory calculus."

Mrs. Detweiler picked up on only one word.

"Guys?" she asked.

"People. Students. Whatever."

"Have you ever visualized yourself in a male role?"

"No."

"Have you parents ever discussed your gender identity with you?"

"Just once. They said if any adults at school ever tried to bully me about it, I should tell them right away."

"Did you feel bullied by adults at school?"

"No. The teachers were nice. They always did their best to help me get ahead."

"Would you rather be judged by your achievements," Mrs. Detweiler asked critically, and then allowed herself an encouraging smile. "Or by the person you are?"

"Both," Mei Lin said in a voice that wondered why she had to pick one or the other.

Mrs. Detweiler went back to her computer. "Your grades qualified you to be a member of the honor society. Have you ever considered the feelings of students who didn't qualify? Perhaps realized that failure might make them feel inferior?"

"It didn't," Mei Lin said confidently. "If you were in the Honor Society, people thought you were some kind of freak."

"Did people call you a freak?"

"I got teased about it sometimes."

"Was there a racial, ethnic or gender based component to that teasing?"

"No. It was just that you were a brain, and brains were freaks."

"Did it occur to you that the teasing might be a defense mechanism to hide feelings of insecurity?"

"No."

Mrs. Detweiler offered her best maternal smile. "I want you to think carefully before you answer, Mei Lin. Please describe the incident related to your ethnicity that had the most profound effect on you. It can be from any time at Franklin High, but it should be in your own words. Please feel free to express your feelings about the incident."

"Stuff happens. I don't let it affect me."

"That's commendable, Mei Lin, but you must have some feelings about what happens."

"I can't control what other people do, but I can always control how I feel about it."

"There are always some outcomes you can't control. Perhaps outside of school while you were attending. Say, for example, if you were turned down for a summer job."

"My parents own a restaurant. I've worked there since I was big enough to bus tables."

"Did your parents instruct or advise you to restrict your responses in this interview? Or in any way attempt to influence what you said?"

"No." The question caught Mei Lin by surprise.

"Mei Lin, I get the impression that you are uncomfortable expressing your feelings."

Mei Lin made eye contact, smiled and said, "I have every right to be a private person."

"I have to tell you, Mei Lin, that unless you can contribute something that will help build a program of diversity, equity and inclusion, I won't be able to incorporate the results of your interview into the study."

"Okay," Mei Lin said. "Was there anything else?"

"No. You may go."

Isobel MacWashington was at the reception desk when Mei Lin came out. Isobel was six feet of café au lait beanpole dressed in a demure skirt and blouse. Her make-up was minimal.

"Hey, Iz," Mei Lin said.

"Muffie? Wow, man, I haven't seen you since--like when was it even?"

"Senior year, Franklin High," Mei Lin said.

"Are you here for this interview thing?" Isobel asked.

"Just finished."

"What's the deal? My folks went ape-shit when they heard I was on the list. Dress for church. Tell the truth. We're here for you no matter what. Like I should have Seal Team Six on speed dial."

"I guess there was some kind of fight at Franklin when we were seniors. One of the girls had a knife."

"Like I'd know anything about that?" Isobel asked. "Someone flashes a shank, I got enough smarts to scram ass out of there."

"I guess people have been suing each other ever since. There was some sort of settlement. The government is supposed to make things better by asking if we were ever discriminated against at school."

"Well, duh. When you're black, you're guilty until proven white. Why would it be any different at Franklin?"

"The woman is going to ask you for specific examples."

"Whoa. I'm one quarter from graduating. I'm starting job interviews. I didn't bust my butt for four years just to have someone ruin it all by hanging a protester sign around my neck."

"Whatever you do, don't tweak this lady. She's wound wa-a-ay too tight."

The receptionist cradled her phone. "Isobel, you can go in now."

END

Breaking News

I'm twenty six years old and my autobiography is nearly finished. I call it *Confessions Of A News Nun*.

Okay, so what's a news nun?

Network news operates on a strict caste system. Permanent employees are the names that scroll past the last five minutes of every Christmas broadcast. Interns are my age, except they have connections. Perma-temps are women with decades of news experience and looks to match. Their job is to keep things running while the permanent employees make creative decisions and screw the interns. Their main tool is the temporary temp, as in yours truly

We're called news nuns because we get about as much time off as we would in a convent. Not that it matters. We aren't paid enough to support a social life.

Becoming a news nun wasn't part of my original career plan. In fact, I landed a broadcast job with a local station right out of journalism school. I saw it as the bottom rung on my personal ladder to success.

Management saw me as the bottom face on the seniority totem pole when they re-shuffled in yet another hopeless attempt to boost ratings. Either I took the hostess job at Angelo's Steak House or came to New York and made the big time in one jump.

"I'll be straight with you," the woman at the temp agency said. "I'm sending you out because I either put a candidate in front of the network or lose the account. You've got no shot at the position, but the Executive

Producer eyeballs every on-camera applicant. You'll pick up some killer interview experience."

So there I was, sitting in front of this stuffed shirt's desk in the ankles-together anchor position radiating as much charisma as I could muster while he scowled through my paperwork.

"Availability?" An Ivy League snarl.

"Immediate," I chirped.

He stabbed the speed dial button on his speaker phone. The temp agency woman was on right quick, kissing up as fast as she could pucker.

"This resume is completely unacceptable," he said.

"We are still searching for the exact match," the woman assured him, "but in the interim I thought--"

"When can she start?"

"Uh, Monday should--"

"She's saying immediate."

"The background check will take seventy two hours, and--"

"Make it happen."

That night I couldn't sleep, so I lay in bed thinking up graceful ways to deflect the amorous celebrities I'd be interviewing.

In my dreams.

Interviews are endless sessions in the hot box, probing for the one answer some producer can use. The six o'clock anchor asks a question to fit the answer. The interviewee comes up split screen and parrots his carefully edited bit. Yours truly is nowhere in sight.

It's been a month of wall to wall fourteen hour days and I'm running on empty. The scary part is I don't want to quit. This is my life's dream. I'm going to die here, like some vacant-eyed junkie looking for one more fix. At least the end of today is in sight. The elevator door to freedom slides open.

Before I can make a dash, the duty perma-temp charges out. "The new intern just blew her cookies prepping for her first on-camera. You'll have to fill in."

Back in the box.

The subject is an ex-cheerleader clinging to a peaches-and-cream complexion into her thirties. Her issue is husbands who work ninety hours a week and abandon their wives in splendid suburban isolation. I think about asking where these dudes hang out, but the rent is due and this isn't a good day to get fired.

Sweet Cheeks is all smiles. She thinks I'm a real newsperson and her crusade is going national. Good luck, Honey. If you were anything but background noise, we wouldn't be doing this in the dead of night.

I'm looking for a way to wrap the session up fast when the door blows open.

Crashing the hot box in the middle of taping means a restart and money down the drain. Major no-no. Unless you're the Executive Producer, with the duty perma-temp in tow.

He takes one look at me and asks, "Is this all you have?"

"Sir," the perma-temp says, "it's almost midnight, and--"

"Get her cleaned up. Get her down to the harbor. Find out where Farrell is shacked up. I want him on top of this situation."

Ed Farrell is a senior correspondent. If he's being assigned, it's big. The producer is gone before I have a chance to ask what it is. The perma-temp is on her cell, trying to calm Sweet Cheeks and track down Farrell at the same time.

The prep crew gang-tackles me. Wardrobe knows my sizes. They shove me into a coat that would take me two years to pay off and a pair of leather dress gloves to die for. Make-up is all over my face and hair, converting me from indoor to outdoor. The sound tech cops a feel while he wires me for remote broadcast.

Then I'm in a jeep with Peter Leong's crew. Peter is the premier network camera. He can make Godzilla look like Gwyneth Paltrow. Top correspondents have screaming matches over who works with him. I upgrade the situation from big to really big.

I still don't know shit. Peter is on his cell. The sound guy is on his cell. I don't dare interrupt the driver. Even at midnight it's not possible to hit seventy in Manhattan but he's doing it anyway, blowing through red lights like he's color-blind.

Near the harbor he threads through a maze of emergency vehicle strobes and leaves rubber stopping at a police barricade. We all hit the ground running. Peter and his guy are lugging sixty pounds of gear apiece and I can barely keep up.

Slippery wooden steps take us down to a pier. The place is already

a news ghetto. People are staring and cameras are pointing. A couple of
hundred yards down the shoreline is another pier, lit up like a shopping
mall opening. Only one boat is tied up there, a cabin cruiser way out at
the end. I see what looks like two people lying on the pier.

Peter hoists the camera to his shoulder and runs out the zoom. "Port
Authority cops," he says.

I suddenly realize how cold the night is.

"Visuals up," Peter announces, and points the lens at me.

"Sound check," I say into my hands-free mike. "Ten-nine-eight-"

"All right," a voice comes through my earpiece. "Got it."

I know the voice. It's no perma-temp. Coverage is being anchored by
Darlene Concannon, goddess of the morning show. I mentally upgrade
from really big to gargantuan.

"Get the camera on the boat," she orders. "Keep it there."

A minute later we see her on the monitor, broadcasting live.

"Responding to an alert from recently installed radiation sensors, a
tactical unit of the Port Authority Police encountered intense automatic
weapons fire from a pleasure boat illegally moored in New York Harbor."

She brings up the view from Peter's camera and goes voice-over about
fears of international terrorists and a dirty bomb. Then she cuts to Ed
Farrell covering a joint announcement by the Mayor, the NYPD and
the FBI.

It lasts about five minutes. Three pompous asses tell however much of
the city is still awake that they're not sure whether the shit has hit the fan
but if it has, no worries. They're all over it.

Yeah. Right.

*   *   *   *   *

Twelve forty AM. The press pier is locked down. No one on or off.
We're all wearing little radiation exposure badges. Ed Farrell is pissed.
We've got the only view of the boat, and he wants it in his background
while he tells the nation how little he knows.

Darlene is taking no prisoners. In the earpiece one minute demanding
facts and cussing like a stevedore when she doesn't get all she wants. The

next minute live on the broadcast monitor; former beauty queen, gracefully aging grandmother, reassuring voice of truth for the nation.

A Nuclear Emergency Response Team is on the road from Washington, video of police escorting a convoy of heavy equipment on semis. An interview with an expert on dirty bombs. How many people could be affected if explosives spread radiation? The news pier is in the 100% zone.

The cabin cruiser is a Chris-Craft, boat-jacked on its way to an antique marine show. No idea who did it, how many are aboard, what they want. I have an epiphany and key my mike.

"Darlene. The son of a bitch is sinking."

"What?" Voice full of rebuke for a news nun daring to interrupt one of her tirades.

"The boat. It's lower in the water than it was when we got here. I know it is."

"Stand by."

*　　*　　*　　*　　*

One ten AM. Ed Farrell is on the monitor comparing the first tapes of the Chris-Craft with the live feed to prove it actually is settling slowly lower in the water. No air time for yours truly.

Unfortunately that's the good news.

One of the people on the boat has been identified. Forget the middle-east. He's an all-American associate professor of nuclear engineering at a big tech school in California. Translation: One of the guys who teach the guys who make real nukes how it's done.

From there it gets worse.

He was an advisor to the long-ago government program back-hauling weapons grade material out of the old Soviet Union. He had access to the real stuff.

Darlene is up with an interviewee who specializes in military nukes.

"Give us an idea of scale," she says. "Could someone make a bomb small enough to fit onto a Chris-Craft?"

"The smallest ever in the US arsenal was a 144 pound suitcase munition that could be carried by three men."

"How much damage could it do?" Darlene asks.

"It could take out the Hoover Dam."

"And the largest? I mean, how big a munition, as you call it, could you cram onto a Chris-Craft?"

"The Mark 83 is a megaton class hydrogen bomb that weighs only 2,400 pounds."

"Damage?"

He's got a lot of data on how much at what radius, but the bottom line is that one of those puppies could scatter Manhattan into the Asteroid Belt.

Next up, another expert with more cheery news.

"The real problem is that if radiation sensors have picked up the signature of the device, then it's leaking, and possibly very dirty."

"Define dirty. Worst case."

More statistics. My take: Don't get caught north of Fort Lauderdale for the next 5,000 years.

*   *   *   *   *

Two seven AM. Four people on the boat. Besides the professor there are a bimbo from the no nukes movement, a former special operations Sergeant who went fruit loops after a tour in Afghanistan and a fishing charter operator whose boat was repoed.

Darlene has a good ear for stereotype. She isn't buying any of that crap. She wants real people, hard details.

What she has is a tape they won't let her broadcast. It scrolls by on the monitor. Three people stand behind the professor while he sits at a table reading from a prepared statement.

".. appalled by the news I see every night. The question facing Americans is not whether their jobs are migrating oversea, or whether they can marry their same sex partners. It's whether they, and the rest of the world, will still be alive tomorrow. And unless the countdown to nuclear Armageddon is stopped, they will not. We must end denial of the nuclear threat as dramatically as the denial of the terrorist threat was ended on 9/11."

He pauses and takes off his glasses. He is through reading. He faces the camera. His voice goes solemn.

"If the salvation of mankind requires the destruction of New York City and all her inhabitants, that is a small enough price to pay."

*   *   *   *   *

Two ten AM. New York isn't like real America. You don't have a bunch of buildings where people work surrounded by suburbs where they live. People live in the City. Whole herds of them.

The stampede is already underway. Shots of the Holland Tunnel and the Verazano Bridge scroll by on the monitor.

Gridlock.

NYPD started out trying to evacuate as many as possible as quickly as possible. As soon as the roads filled, they were over-ruled by Homeland Security. Checkpoints. Stop every car. Can't risk a secondary terrorist strike on a major transportation artery.

Your tax dollars at work.

I understand the people who have abandoned umpty-gazillion dollar SUVs to make a walk for it. The ones I don't get are the crowds that have formed on the streets above the harbor, watching in silent fascination.

The camera pans and stops on a man. He holds a sleepy three-year old still in her jammies under a winter coat. The boy who clings to the man's pant leg stares with wide five-year old eyes.

My mind is screaming at the guy. *You fucking idiot. This is the real deal. Get your kids out of harm's way. Start walking. You might just make it.*

*   *   *   *   *

Two twenty five AM. The police escort two men to the end of the news pier. Nondescript. Jeans and parkas. They could have come from any factory shift. They train huge binoculars on the Chris-Craft.

"D-Boys," someone says.

I look at Peter.

"Delta Force commandos," he explains.

"Do they think they can take down the boat before The Nutty Professor puts us all in orbit?"

"Armies," Peter says, "are constantly training to fight the last war. The next one always catches them by surprise."

I alert Darlene to what's going on. She wants to know if a decision has been made. Apparently there is a huge turf war raging. Every Government agency with anything resembling a tactical response unit wants a share of the limelight.

"Aren't they negotiating?" I ask.

"Probably. An FCC goon squad shut down our scanning gear to make sure we can't pick up any chatter on the tactical frequencies."

*   *   *   *   *

Two thirty AM. Ed Farrell again. In the background a white step van is making its way through a maze of emergency vehicle strobes.

"...Nuclear Emergency Response Team truck has arrived on the scene," he says as it moves out of camera range. "The authorities appear to be positioning it where it can move in quickly if the situation permits."

No one seems to be saying what the situation is. Farrell obviously doesn't know, and Darlene is in my earpiece getting on his case about that.

"Save it for the junior staff," Farrell tells her. "I'm hearing the news operation is moving to Washington. What is the evacuation plan?"

"You listen to me, you puffed-up little shit. If you try to wimp out, you'll never broadcast again."

Our sound guy gets on his cell to the other crew to ask if Hair-Head Ed has sent out for fresh spankies, but it's only bravado. Darlene has just told all of us we're not going anywhere.

"Witness may not sound very heroic," Peter tells me, "but this story has to be told."

I shiver inside the network's expensive coat. At least I'll go out looking good.

*   *   *   *   *

Three AM. Pictures on the monitor. The warehouse where they made the bomb. Floodlights. White step vans. People in white moon suits.

Darlene interviewing another expert. If the warehouse is dirty, the professor is probably paranoid from radiation exposure. He could cook off his nuke any time. Even if he and the others can be overpowered, the Nuclear Emergency response team will have to move fast. He may have it on a timer. And carefully. He certainly has it booby trapped to blow if anyone touches it.

Former head of the Nuclear Emergency Response Team. The Team is trained to deal with booby traps. His mantra: Gain control of the situation, disarm the munition, dispose of the waste.

Former FBI tactical response specialist. Tough call. The people on the cabin cruiser seem to have their buoyancy issues contained. But if the boat starts sinking again, they could pull the trigger. Fatigue has to be taking its toll. Four people, incomplete psychological profiles, each letting out an individual cry for attention. If group integrity breaks down, you have four potential fingers on the button.

Decision time. If they are going to raid the Chris-Craft, it has to be now. Between three and four AM. Low point in the human biological clock.

Darlene is in the earpiece, telling Peter to have his low-light gear ready to go in case they douse the floods. Then she goes off at me.

"If we lose lights, you'll have to narrate. You will be the only one in a position to see anything. The entire nation will be depending on you for the story. Do you understand?"

"Yes," I blurt, and then manage to choke out, "I'm ready."

I remember the new intern blowing her cookies prepping for her first on-camera. It's a good thing I haven't eaten for a while.

*   *   *   *   *

Three eleven AM. Darlene has nailed it. The lights go out. I hear myself describing the scene, thinking slow down, speak clearly.

"We have two, no three, boats. Powerful motors. We can hear them approaching. Now machine gun fire coming from the cabin cruiser. Red tracer bullets."

They look green on the monitor. Peter has the low light equipment running. I see the boats, see them turn away. I'm thinking *Omigod; it's a cluster fuck* when a rapid series of explosions erupts from the cabin cruiser.

"Concussion grenades," I tell the world, snatching something I overhear another reporter say. "The movement on the water was a diversion. Delta Force commandos are storming the boat from the pier."

The pier is darker than the hallway in my apartment building and I haven't got a fucking clue who is doing what, but I actually sound like I know what I'm talking about as I describe a fierce exchange of point-blank automatic gunfire aboard the Chris-Craft.

Silence.

It comes abruptly and takes everyone by surprise. I realize I need to be narrating.

"It seems to be over," I say, thinking it sounds stupid, and then remembering that my voice is the camera. "It seems to be over and now we're just waiting."

Either there's going to be a nuclear explosion or there isn't. Then a flicker from the pier.

"Lights," I hear myself say, and the floods come on full. "The lights on the pier are back on."

I describe guys in Army Kevlar on the Chris-Craft. They haul two bodies up and throw them onto the pier. Armored soldiers with medical bags rush on board. An NYPD cruiser has started down the pier with its strobes on. Behind it rolls a convoy of humvees and a white step van.

Peter has the whole thing on the monitor now. In what must be the ultimate violation of the Network caste system, Darlene actually thanks me *by name* before she takes over narrating what the viewers see.

Soldiers carrying stretchers off the Chris-Craft, loading them onto humvees, getting the hell out of there while the people in white moonsuits take over.

My heart is rolling thunder inside my chest. I've just had my first national exposure, and our side has won.

Peter winks at me. "Round one to the good guys."

That's when it hits me. I'm looking across New York Harbor at nuclear devastation still waiting to happen.

Darlene is in the earpiece, squabbling with the producer over which expert she gets to use. The producer wins. She goes with the cheap guy. The best in the country isn't worth the extra ten grand. Nuclear bombs are nuclear bombs, and the audience doesn't know one PhD from another.

I don't know how anybody can be asshole enough to look for money at a time like this, but it doesn't seem to bother the guy Darlene's got on.

He's talking about how nuclear bombs work. High explosives drive segments of nuclear material into a critical mass. The first perceivable energy release is an intense flash of light, then the blast waves followed by umpty thousand degree heat. All in less than a heartbeat.

I'm watching the Moonsuits carrying boxes of gear aboard the Chris-Craft and into the cabin. Darlene asks the asshole to describe what the Nuclear Response people are doing in the boat.

"Cramped quarters will be the most difficult issue," he says. "The team will need to get all the potential triggers disarmed and the munition stabilized before removal can begin."

"How do you remove something like that?" Darlene asks. "I mean, that has to be tremendously dangerous."

"Step one is probably to secure flotation devices on the boat. Then it can be towed out to sea. It will probably be hoisted onto a barge. It may be possible to disassemble the boat from around the bomb. Or the whole thing may have to be cased in lead and concrete and simply sunk in the deepest available water. It all depends on what the Nuclear Emergency Response Team finds."

He makes it sound like someone has thought this scenario through in advance. Like there is a plan in place. There are fallback options. There are resources available and people ready to execute on command.

That's not the feeling I'm getting watching the pier across the way. A second white Step Van arrives. One of the Moonsuits has made three trips out onto the dock to talk to someone on a phone in the first truck.

"Can you tell us what we are seeing?" Darlene asks the asshole. "Why the phone calls?"

"It may be that the man who built the bomb survived the assault. If so, the head of the Nuclear Emergency Response Team will certainly want to forward questions to him."

"What if he gives them the wrong answers?" Darlene asks. "Intentionally wrong."

"The men and women on the Team have been exhaustively prepared. Their training and experience will tell them if they are getting wrong information."

I hope so. The sun is a red glow on the horizon now, and the monitor shows a camera pan of the crowd above the harbor. More pans of outlying neighborhoods. It's an unreal sight. Maybe a hundred thousand people. Maybe more. Way too many for the cops to move. Nothing to do but let them mill around.

Then it happens.

The Moonsuits come scrambling out of the cabin cruiser and onto the pier, making for their truck. The press pier goes silent.

Something has gone terribly wrong.

My mind screams at me to run. If the Moonsuits are running, there must be a chance. But that's just me clinging to a last vestige of hope.

The asshole was right about one thing. The flash is killer awesome.

END

Printed in the United States
by Baker & Taylor Publisher Services